THE GULAG RATS

Punishment Battalion Series
Book Four

Charles Whiting
writing as
K N Kostov

SAPERE
BOOKS

THE GULAG RATS

Published by Sapere Books.

24 Trafalgar Road, Ilkley, LS29 8HH

saperebooks.com

ISBN: 978-0-85495-595-4

Partake my confidence! No creature's made so mean
But that, some way, it boasts, could we investigate,
Its supreme worth: fulfils, by ordinance of fate
Its momentary task, gets glory all its own,
Tastes triumph in the world, pre-eminent, alone.

Robert Browning, Fifine at the Fair XXIX

The Gulag Archipelago was the name given to the great system of concentration camps spread across Soviet Russia during the days of the dictator, Josef Stalin.

SECRET!

ATTENTION: COMMANDERS, 2nd WHITE RUSSIAN FRONT, 1st WHITE RUSSIAN FRONT, 1st UKRAINIAN FRONT.

STAVKA GENERAL ORDER FOR FIELD PUNISHMENT BATTALIONS.

1. Punishment will be carried out at the front. It will consist of the most arduous and dangerous tasks, such as minefield clearance, burying dead and laying roads under fire, assault attacks on fortified enemy positions etc.

2. Conditions of punishment. Reduced rate of pay, uniform without badges of rank, unit insignia. Food on a scale three rating. Parcels from the Homeland will not be handed out. Officers empowered to hand over personal mail at their own discretion. Association with other troops or civilians strictly forbidden.

3. Duration of punishment. Death in action or maximum of six months of active service at the front. Thereafter the soldier criminal is to be returned to his parent unit.

ATTENTION: None of the above conditions apply to Punishment Battalion 333! In the case of the 333, on the criminal's death his records will be returned to Central Records stamped KIA where they will be destroyed by the officer in charge. The above ruling applies to those of officer rank in the 333 up to and including the colonel commanding.

Stavka HQ 1 June 1944

BOOK ONE: *MARCH TO THE VISTULA*

CHAPTER 1

On the horizon the German guns continued to thunder. But the barrage was moving away to another part of the Russian line. The Germans had broken the Russian attack; they were wasting no more shells here.

The colonel tipped his cap to the back of his big head and wiping the thick pearls of greasy sweat from his red, angry face, surveyed the scene.

At the side of the road a T-34 tank lay blown on its side in the middle of an orchard, ripe apples lying all around its still smoking tracks. One of its crew, almost naked, hung in one of the trees like some monstrous human fruit, a chunk of steel nearly a metre long thrust through his pale stomach.

On the road itself lay the dead of his own command, Punishment Battalion 333, sprawled out in the extravagant gestures of those violently done to death: an old man with the shaven head of the long-term gulag rat, still clutching a looted bottle of Polish vodka in his dirty paw; an officer hit and burst apart by a shell like a ripe marrow; a boy, perhaps fifteen or sixteen, but a gulag rat all the same. His clenched fists were buried in the grey, obscene snake of his guts, his teeth bared, as if in the moment of his death he had still been trying to thrust back the entrails. Next to him, a sergeant, his upper body stripped to the rib cage which glittered in the early summer sun like polished ivory.

At his side on the road Vulf, the little, bespectacled intellectual who had been with the colonel ever since '41 when the Punishment Battalion had been formed from the inmates of Stalin's prison camps, did not look at the dead from the attack which had just failed. In the last three years he had seen enough slaughter. Instead he looked at the big colonel, taking in the harshly handsome and masterful face, marred only by a trace of bitterness around the mouth, and wondered again at the change that had come over him since he had taken over the command of the gulag rats.

Once the colonel, with the curly dark hair now going a little grey, had been a hero of the Soviet Union, a marshal and an army commander. Then he had run foul of the Soviet dictator, Stalin, and had been sent to the camps, his career ruined, his wife dead — a suicide — his son God knows where. When they had been released from the camps in '41 to save Moscow from the German attack, he had hated Stalin and everything his regime stood for. Now he was as loyal as the rest of them, seemingly blind to the fact that the Red Army was no longer defending Mother Russia. Instead it was invading that part of Poland over which Stalin and the archenemy, Hitler had conspired to take from Poland in 1939. Why, Vulf asked himself, why? Patriotism or conformism? The colonel had seen enough. He swung round and looked back at the positions the battalion had taken up after they had broken and run.

'Vulf,' he commanded harshly.

'Comrade colonel?'

The colonel slapped his cane angrily against the side of his boot, the muscles twitching at the side of his hard face. 'Let's get back to that bunch of cowards and begin the slaughter...'

The colonel stood on the back of a truck and stared at his battalion lined up raggedly in front of him in the farmyard of the abandoned Polish farm. The gulag rats were all sorts. Political prisoners like he had once been, criminals, sexual perverts. Nobility and scum mixed together. He saw strength on the faces of his men who stared straight ahead, glaring at the far horizon still held by the Fritzes in spite, of their bloody sacrifice. He saw weakness there too — the mediocre weakness of body and spirit of those who would always run with the crowd. And he smelt the rancid sweat of cowardice from those who had led the rush for the rear once the Fritzes had begun throwing lead poisoning their way.

Angrily he tossed away his long cigarette and, raising his voice so that they could all hear it in spite of the barrage, barked: 'You are gulag rats. There are saints and heroes among you, I know. There are also crooks and cowards, too.'

In the front rank Senior Captain Vassily, a rough, blood-stained bandage wrapped round his corn-coloured hair, dropped his gaze to the dust, as if he, personally, were ashamed of what had happened that morning. 'But whatever you are,' the colonel continued, 'I didn't think you were fools.' His harsh face contorted into a sneer. 'Did you think that you, scum released from the camps to atone for your crimes and your worthless lives here at the front, could run away from the slaughter just like that? By the Holy Virgin of Kazan it is not possible that gulag rats could be *that* stupid!' He stretched out his arm and pointed to the fir forest to his rear, his hand, scarred by the sabre cuts of old wars, trembling with hardly suppressed rage. 'Those trees are filled with the gentlemen of the green cross, armed with machine-guns. Do you think they would have allowed rabble like you to run any further? Of course, you can't be allowed to contaminate ordinary good folk. You have only one future — *march or croak*! They would have shot down every last one of you cowardly pigs!'

'They can't shoot all of us, comrade colonel,' someone grumbled. The colonel swung round angrily. It was Sergeant Alexei, his bearded old face a mixture of resentment and anger.

'What did you say, little brother?' he asked with deceptive softness.

The sergeant, who had been with the colonel from the beginning and had won two Orders of the Soviet Union in spite of once killing a *politcommissar* in a brawl, repeated his statement.

'Ay ... ay...' others agreed with the veteran. 'Those sons-of-whores can't kill all of us... Yes, let's kill those green-cross pigs. They're worse than the Fritzes!'

The colonel made a quick decision. 'Starting with Sergeant Alexei, number off in twenties. Every twentieth man, officer, NCO or simple soldier will then step forward.' He slapped his hand on his pistol holster as if he might enforce his command with its help. Puzzled and reluctant, the gulag rats started to count off the twenties until the colonel was satisfied he had enough victims.

'Forward march!' he bellowed.

Near the wall, a waiting Vulf nodded to the three senior sergeants, trusted men all of them, positioned behind the machine-guns. They returned his nod and jerked back the cocking bolts, as the twenty or so gulag rats singled out by the colonel stumbled forward over the rough cobbles of the yard.

At their head Sergeant Alexei came to a halt, knowing what the colonel was about to do. 'Comrade colonel, you can't!' he cried. 'No, not to us, the ones who fought and didn't run!'

'Colonel,' Senior Captain Vassily added his voice to the suddenly ashen-faced NCO's. 'Some of those men were the bravest fighters of the whole regiment.'

The colonel looked down at him, his blue eyes icy. 'Innocent and guilty, they must suffer all, Vassily. That is the only kind of discipline gulag rats understand.'

Vassily looked at him aghast, his mouth opened stupidly. 'But you … you.'

Vulf, pistol in his hand, eyes composed, even cynical behind the thick horn-rimmed glasses, ordered them to line up against the wall.

Numbly, some of them sobbing like stricken children, they did as they were ordered, followed by the wary-eyed machine-gunners.

The colonel raised his voice. 'I herewith sentence you all to death for cowardice in the face of the enemy in battle. That sentence will be carried out at once. Politcommissar Vulf, you —'

His words were drowned by a scream of crazed rage. A soldier in the front rank dropped his rifle and bolted forward. Vassily tried to stop him. Too late! He was running directly for the colonel, screaming obscenities, spittle dribbling down the coal-black stubble of his unshaven jaw.

The colonel waited with apparent calmness. Then just as the crazy soldier almost reached him, he dropped to the ground on one knee, tucked in his head and reached up. The soldier hurtled through the air over the colonel's head and slammed down on the cobbles — *hard*. The colonel chopped his hand down hard on the prostrate man's exposed throat. He went limp suddenly, head hanging to one side. Vulf looked across the courtyard at the colonel, who did not seem even to be breathing hard.

The colonel shook his head. They had selected enough victims.

Vulf swung round. 'Machine-gunners,' he commanded in a thin, affected, almost feminine voice, 'take aim!'

There was a tense hush among the watching soldiers.

Against the wall, some of the wretched victims fell on their knees and raised their hands in the classic pose of supplication. Sergeant Alexei crossed himself and started to pray softly.

Vulf waited till the gunners were ready, their mates holding up the long belts of gleaming yellow slugs, ready to feed them into the guns' breeches; then he brought his right hand down sharply and screamed: '*Fire!*'

The heavy machine-guns burst into frenetic activity, the gunners swinging them back and forth, riddling the men with slugs, slamming them against the wall, forcing them to their knees, smashing them back and forth, lower and lower until they lay in the bloody scuffed dirt. Heaped bodies twitched for a few moments more as the gunners, crazed with blood-lust now, kept pumping slugs into them till Vulf was crying, '*Ceasefire ... for God's sake, ceasefire...*'

There was a loud echoing silence which seemed to go on for ever until the colonel broke it with a dry incisive, 'Punishment Battalion 333 will dismiss... Company commanders will report to me on the hour... We attack the Fritzes again in battalion strength,' he paused and glanced at his watch momentarily, 'at exactly fourteen hundred hours this afternoon!'

He waited, as if he expected some comment from the silent battalion. But there was none. The gulag rats were awed into silence and obedience. He flashed a final glance at the pile of murdered men lying below the farm wall, pocked as if with some loathsome skin disease, and commanded: 'Get some of this shit-shovelling scum to clear away the mess.'

With that he walked back to the farmhouse kitchen which served as his HQ. Behind him a boy started to sob broken-heartedly...

CHAPTER 2

But the penal battalion was not fated to attack that particular day. At one o'clock, sixty minutes before the gulag rats were scheduled to go in once more, Vulf, running into the farm kitchen where the colonel was studying the map for a last time, cried out, 'Comrade colonel ... comrade colonel ... *it's him!*'

The colonel swung round to stare at a red-faced, wildly excited Vulf. 'Who?' he demanded.

'The marshal... The commander of the First Belorussian Front!'

'Marshal Rokossovsky!' the colonel, exclaimed. 'What in three devils' name is he doing so far forward? Doesn't he know that people get killed up here?'

'I don't know, comrade colonel,' Vulf answered, raising his voice above the noise of vehicles driving into the entrance of the little Polish farmyard. 'But here he is!'

The colonel flung a glance through the dirty, flyblown window. It was Rokossovsky, all right. There was no mistaking that pale, cynical face with the inevitable cigarette stuck in the side of his broad, humorous mouth. He sat there in the back of his open Mercedes next to a plump blonde pigeon, who wore the earth-brown tunic of a member of the Red Army — obviously his current mistress.

The colonel grabbed his cap and snapped, 'Come on, you little intellectual shit, let us go and greet the great man!'

As the Mercedes came to a halt and the staff cars filled with officers and guards swung to left and right, watched by bemused gulag rats, the colonel snapped to attention, hand raised to his cap in an immaculate salute.

Marshal Rokossovsky deigned not to notice him. Instead he popped another sticky chocolate into the open mouth of his mistress and then pressed his lips to her plump white hand. 'Arrogant swine,' the colonel told himself, amused. 'But then the marshal has always been an arrogant swine.'

Finally Rokossovsky raised his right hand in a languid salute, no sign of recognition on his face.

The colonel dropped his arm and waited. The marshal let him wait as he dismissed his staff and gave the bodyguard their instructions. Finally he was ready. 'Colonel,' he said with cold formality as if they had never shovelled shit together back in '38 or washed each other's foot rags when one or other of them had been sick with typhus, 'I must speak with you privately. Dismiss — er — that.' He waved a white, well-manicured hand at Vulf.

The colonel did so and then, at a suitable distance, followed the marshal towards his HQ, noting Rokossovsky's purposeful, masterly stride and remembering the times when the two of them had trudged wearily through the deep snow, urged on by the knouts of the Cossack guards, their progress marked by the bloody shit of dysentery that dripped down their legs.

At the door the marshal waited.

The colonel sprang forward and opened it for him. Only then did the marshal proceed. The colonel closed the door behind him. Now what, he wondered.

Suddenly Rokossovsky turned round, a huge grin on his face, his arms extended. 'Come to me, you gulag rat!' he cried.

The colonel advanced on him and they hugged each other, pressing warm kisses on their hard soldiers' faces, slapping one another's back in sheer delight, repeating the old phrase over and over again, *'gulag rat ... gulag rat...'*

They wiped their eyes and looked at each other, trying to assess the toll extracted by the years since they had both entered the camps as 'traitors' to the Soviet cause, to be released only when 'Old Leather Face' — the Red Army's nickname for the Soviet dictator, Stalin — had needed them.

'Have you a little water for me, brother?' Rokossovsky asked, sitting on the edge of the rough kitchen table.

'Of course, little brother,' the colonel responded and fetching a bottle of pepper-vodka and two glasses, poured one for each of them before handing the marshal the salt-cellar.

In silence the two of them put salt on the 'V' of skin made by extending their thumbs and forefingers, licked it off and then downed their vodka with a swift '*Nastrovya pan!*'

For a while the two of them chatted about old times when they had been brigade commanders in the Far East Army before they had been arrested and sent to the camps. Then the marshal sighed and said, 'I no longer dream of the stars, little brother. I carry out my heavy tasks for Mother Russia and forget that I am keeping Old Leather Face in power.' He shrugged. 'What else can one do?'

The colonel nodded. 'I prefer no longer to think of such things, comrade marshal —'

'*Brother!*'

'*Brother.* I live for the day, do my duty as a Russian soldier and hope that all will come out right in the end.'

'Exactly.' Abruptly Rokossovsky put down his glass, his pale face a little flushed with the alcohol now, but business-like again. 'All right, the reason for my visit, brother? This. I have a mission for your gulag rats.'

'We have one. Out there.' He indicated through the window to where the horizon burnt once more with the Fritz barrage.

Rokossovsky shook his head. 'Let Konev's infantry take care of that little problem. We're moving further north.'

'Warsaw?' the colonel guessed crudely.

The marshal beamed. 'You haven't lost your cunning, little brother,' he exclaimed. 'You'd make a good general.'

'You forget. I was one — longer than you.'

Rokossovsky ignored the comment, his face serious now. 'Marshal Stalin has ordered me and the First Belorussian Front to attack towards Praga on the opposite side of the River Vistula to Warsaw. We are expected to achieve our objective between the fifth and eighth of August and begin seizing bridgeheads on the western bank of the river.'

'I can see Old Leather Face's reasoning,' the colonel said thoughtfully. 'The vital traffic arteries running north-south and east-west cross Warsaw. If the Fritzes are going to keep control of the Eastern Front, they've got to keep Warsaw.'

'Exactly. After all that's where the Red Army failed in 1920, when we were both young captains down here. Pilsudski managed to hang on to Warsaw and that was the end of our hopes of ever conquering Poland.' He cleared his throat. 'Now I can imagine you are asking yourself — what has all this got to do with me and my gulag rats?'

'Something like that.'

'Well, little brother, when I heard it was you who was in charge of the 333rd Penal Battalion, I knew you were the man I needed.'

'To do what?'

'To lead the drive for Praga,' Rokossovsky answered. 'You are no fool, no glory hunter, no waster of men. If anyone can get to Praga first it will be you and your gulag rats.'

'First?' the colonel queried puzzled.

Rokossovsky laughed cynically. 'Yes, first. I know Old Leather Face and have absolutely no trust in him. Today he tells me that I shall have the honour of leading the drive of the Red Army to the Vistula. Tomorrow in order to spur me on he'll tell that so-called Marshal Konev' — he spat contemptuously on the floor — '*the fat swine*, to take his First Ukrainian Front and drive for the Vistula too. It will be Stalin's usual tactic. Setting one man against another, knowing that marshals run wars as if it were a matter of personal glory.'

'Is it?' the colonel queried, half-serious, half-amused.

Rokossovsky, eyebrows wrinkled as if he were giving the question serious consideration, then said, 'When this war is successfully concluded, little brother, those who have won victories will command great power. I want to be one of those who wield the power within the Red Army.' Rokossovsky lowered his voice and looked quickly to left and right in case he was being overheard.

The colonel told himself that even a marshal of the Soviet Union with over half a million men under his command was still afraid of the long arm of Beria, the feared head of the secret police, the NKVD.

'For one day, little brother, there will be a reckoning with that pock-faced swine in the Kremlin and I, for one, have a few old debts from the days of the camps to repay. But enough of that.' He raised his voice. 'This is what I want you to do. I want you to avoid combat as much as possible. Sneak your way through the Fritz line if you can.'

'But we are infantry, brother,' the colonel objected. 'We need armoured support, motor transport to lead an advance of that kind!'

Rokossovsky grinned. 'You were, brother. *You were!* A battalion of the latest T-34s is on its way to help you. And if my ancient ears don't deceive me, here is your transport coming in now.' He gestured to the window and the colonel stared in open-mouthed amazement, as the first dust-covered American lease-lend truck eased its way into the farmyard.

'But how did you know I would accept the mission, brother?' the colonel stuttered, as more and more of the American trucks braked to a stop.

Rokossovsky smiled. 'I trusted you as a fellow gulag rat. Besides, I could have sent you back to the gulag if you refused, you know? It's still full of field-grade officers.'

Now it was the colonel's turn to grin; he gave the marshal the full benefit of his stainless steel teeth. 'You bastard, you haven't changed!' he exclaimed.

'That's why I'm a marshal of the Soviet Union again and you're still a colonel commanding a bunch of prison scum after three years of war.' The marshal's grin vanished and he placed his big hand on the colonel's shoulder in a mixture of affection and alarm. 'Remember, little brother, it's bandit country out there on the road to Warsaw. There are the Fritzes, but there are Ukrainian renegades, too, fighting for themselves and the Fritzes. There are Poles of all shades of opinion, *our* Poles, the Fritzes' Poles and *their* own Poles. Every man's hand will be against you and...' he hesitated momentarily.

'Go on,' the colonel urged, intrigued by this sudden mission which had been thrust upon his gulag rats after their miserable failure of the morning.

The cynical light had vanished from Marshal Rokossovsky's eyes to be replaced by a look of concern, almost of sadness. 'And if you fail, little brother, Old Leather Face will have you sent back to the Gulag Archipelago — or worse...'

CHAPTER 3

A summer-dry twig cracked underfoot.

'Son-of-a-bitch!' Captain Vassily hissed angrily, 'that man, watch your shit-feet!'

The gulag rat muttered under his breath, but he parted the bushes, and allowed Vassily to pass through. One by one, half of the company, led by the senior captain, sneaked by under the light of the stars.

Vassily paused. Ahead of them lay the village held, according to intelligence, by a company of over-age Fritzes from one of their stomach battalions. He studied it for a moment. It was the usual collection of small Polish cottages grouped around an onion-towered church. They'd have their lookouts up in the tower, of course, and the first cottages would be fortified. He'd have to go in from the rear.

Swiftly he made his dispositions, ending with, 'And watch your shit feet. Anyone who alarms those Fritzes before we reach the village will have to answer to me. I'll have the nuts off'n him with a piece of broken glass. Now off you go. And remember, the colonel has ordered that *no one* is to escape!'

It had been the colonel's plan to attack just here at the Polish village. The tanks would need a road leading west and the village blocked the entry into a second-class country road which did just that. Once the village was taken, again according to *Stavka* intelligence, there would be little in the way of organized Fritz resistance to stop them in their dash towards Praga. But Vassily told himself bitterly that they had to capture the village first and ensure none of the Fritz cripples got away to spread the news of a breakthrough. Everything was up to him and his half company of gulag rats.

Now the two files of men crept through the silver darkness, dodging in and out of the trees that bordered the village, fingers clutched nervously on the triggers of their weapons as they spread out on both flanks, ready to open fire at the first sign that they had been spotted.

Once, somewhere off to the right, a flare hissed into the air, startling them, making their hearts thump like triphammers as they froze in its eerie white glare, until it sank to the ground like a falling angel and everything was dark again. 'Nervous people, the Fritzes,' Vassily said to himself under his breath. 'Always firing off flares in the middle of the night. Must have plenty of them.'

Now they were close enough to the little cottages to make out their outlines fairly clearly and Captain Vassily could smell that typical Fritz odour: a compound of black tobacco and Fritz sweat. The place was occupied, all right. 'Crawl!' he whispered. 'Pass it on — *crawl!*'

His men bent and started to crawl through the long grass at the edge of the village, nostrils full of its warm summer odour, taking their time, knowing that if the old men of the Fritz stomach battalion spotted them now, only a hundred metres from their gun muzzles, they would be done for.

The church disappeared into the silver gloom to their rear. Vassily led his men ever closer to the village. It could only be a matter of minutes now, he knew, before they were spotted. But by that time he wanted to be in a position to rush the defenders from the rear.

Suddenly it happened. The hectic, hysterical gaggle of geese. 'Damn Polack geese!' he cried. 'Every shitting Polack village has them!' He sprang to his feet as the chatter of the geese was followed by the first hoarse cry of alarm in German, and yelled: 'Charge ... *to the attack!*'

'Urrah!' the gulag rats burst into a roar as they raced forward into the village street, the geese cackling and squawking at their running feet, the first wild stabs of scarlet flame cutting the darkness.

'*Davoi ... davoi!*' Captain Vassily urged frantically as a fat German, clad only in his underwear and jack-boots loomed up out of the darkness. Instinctively he pressed the trigger of his submachine-gun. The Fritz screamed, his hands clutching frantically at his ripped-open stomach. 'Save you bothering about stomach powder anymore, Fritz!' Vassily roared heartlessly as he pelted by.

A German leaned out of an upstairs window, rifle clutched in fat hands. A gulag rat fired. The German yelped and fell out of the window. He hit the ground like a sack of wet cement.

A machine-gun burred in high-pitched hysteria. Tracer, red and white, zipped through the darkness like a swarm of angry hornets. Behind Vassily half a dozen gulag rats skidded to a stop, dropped their weapons, and hit the cobbles in a mess of twitching limbs.

Vassily didn't hesitate. He grabbed the grenade tucked down the side of his boot and flung it towards the M.G. pit. It exploded with a flash of blinding white light. Vassily ducked and heard the shrapnel pattering down on his helmet like heavy summer rain on a tin roof. A head rolled to a stop at his feet like a football abandoned by some careless child. It bore a Hitler-type moustache. '*Heil Hitler!*' he cried and ran on.

A knife hissed through the air. Behind Vassily a man yelped and went down, clutching his shoulder with fingers through which the blood jetted in bright scarlet spurts.

Then they were in the cottages, slaughtering the Fritzes. An officer rushed at Vassily, dressed only in his underwear, his teeth bared in anger, hands clutching at the Russian's throat. Vassily launched a kick at his guts — and missed. The Fritz's sausage-fingers fastened on his neck. Vassily tried in vain to break his grip, red and white stars exploding in front of his eyes. The officer's garlic laden breath assailed his nostrils as Vassily writhed back and forth, choking for air, attempting frantically to free himself, clawing at the Fritz's shoulders, ripping skin and cotton from them.

His ears started to pop. The blackness, charged with bright scarlet, threatened to overcome him. Instinctively his hands felt down below the Fritz's gut and found his genitals, soft, heavy and yielding. He didn't hesitate. He would be out in another moment. He twisted with the last of his remaining strength. The Fritz screamed high, shrill. The grip on Vassily's neck relaxed. He did not wait for a second invitation. His right elbow slammed into the Fritz's gasping mouth. The officer's false teeth plopped obscenely out of his mouth in the same instant that a gulag rat's bayonet sank deep between his shoulders. The Fritz's officer cap dropped to the ground.

Vassily lay on the cobbles next to him, while his men raced forward to the foremost cottages and the church, firing from the hip as they ran, shooting down those of the stomach battalion who attempted to surrender. Then they began their looting. This was the only reward that the gulag rats expected for daily risking their miserable lives for a Russia that had sentenced them to the camps and a slow death.

It was in the midst of the looting, that the senior sergeant reported to a groggy Vassily that there was a 'dying Polack' in the village. 'Seems to be some sort of holy water shaker to me, comrade captain,' he explained hoarsely, tilting back his head and letting the *korn* run into his parched throat. 'Dressed up in a black frock like all those holy shits.'

'What happened?' Vassily demanded, sitting up.

'Thought he was a Fritz sniper in the church. So we blasted the poor shit in the guts.' The sergeant shrugged easily. 'Still, it doesn't matter, comrade senior captain. After all, he's only a Polack, ain't he?'

Captain Vassily said nothing. Instead he raised himself and ignoring the fact that a bunch of already drunken gulag rats were bayoneting screaming Fritzes at the wall next to the church, he crossed over to where the priest lay dying on the steps of his church, arms spread out as if he were Jesus on the Cross himself.

The burst of bullets had caught the elderly Pole in his belly and there were neat holes, like those stitched for buttons, ripped across the tight black cloth of his robe, blood welling in little red bubbles from each one. He saw the officer approaching. There was no fear in his eyes, nor the goodness one might expect from a priest. Instead the look was of hard burning hatred, as he cried in Polish, 'May God's curse be upon you red pigs, and on your sons and their sons!' He groaned, and dark red blood began to trickle from his suddenly pinched nostrils. 'Why can't you leave us alone, you Russians and Germans? What have we Poles done? Why must we be tortured thus ... for centuries?'

'Because we are Poles,' Captain Vassily answered in Polish, bending down to look more closely at the priest's terrible wounds and seeing he had no chance.

The priest stared at him knowingly, as the life ebbed from him rapidly. '*You...?*'

Vassily nodded in silence.

The priest grabbed the captain's hand with surprising strength, his face frantic. 'Then say the last rites. Give me them!' he demanded. 'You can do it, even as a layman, if you are one of us … *please*!' Tears trickled down his ashen face. 'I beg you!'

Reluctantly Vassily took off his helmet and knelt on one knee. The priest sighed, as if with relief, and fell back, closing his eyes, his fat hands clasped in prayer, the blood welling from his ruined body.

Vassily commenced a little awkwardly, trying to remember the words that he had been forced to forget so long ago, while at his side the priest's lips moved softly in the responses, a look of infinite calm now on his dying face.

Thus it was that Vulf and Captain Weis of the Second Company, as they drove up with the T-34s, spotted Vassily kneeling without his helmet, holding the dead priest's hand.

'What in three devils' name has got into him?' Weis demanded as the infantry started to drop off the tanks ready to move up the road towards the west.

Vulf took in the scene, but all he said to the dark-bearded, hook-nosed Volga-German Weis was a cynical: 'Perhaps our young friend has just fallen in love with him. He looks rather nice in his black frock.'

Weis snorted and then started bawling out orders. Thirty minutes later the point of Punishment Battalion was on its way again. The Fritz line had been penetrated. Now the River Vistula and Warsaw, their objective, lay less than one hundred kilometres to the west.

Above them in the hills which surrounded the village, the Ukrainian put down his night glasses and rolled over on his back to stare upwards at the evil-bearded, one-eyed features of the Gorilla and said, 'It's the Russians all right, chief. They've broken through.'

The Gorilla tugged at his eye-patch and listened to the roar of the trucks which were following the tanks down below. Then he grunted. 'Easy pickings, Eugen. We'll let the Fritzes have the bodies... We'll get the loot.'

Eugen laughed. It was not a pleasant sound.

CHAPTER 4

'*Heaven, arse and cloudburst!*' *Standartenführer* Kass exclaimed angrily and tossed the message to the floor. 'I'd give my shitting right arm to be fighting on the Western Front instead of on this damned midden!' The big SS commander, his face scarred with sabre cuts from his student days in Vienna, glared at his chief-of-staff. 'Well, what do you think, Hans? Do you think it's reliable?'

'I tried to raise the village by radio immediately I received the message; there was no reply. I sent out a dispatch rider to check in person. He has not come back.' The chief-of-staff eased the monocle which he affected, as if it gave him some pain to keep it in position in his right eye. 'Needless to say there was no air recce coming from the Luftwaffe.'

The big SS general grunted. 'As usual. All that Fat Hermann's boys are useful for is propping up some expensive bar in Warsaw or playing with themselves. Let the stupid SS get their turnips shot off. They've got far more important things to do.' He controlled himself with difficulty.

Outside they were shooting the latest batch of prisoners from the Polish Home Army, lining them up in batches of six, allowing them to say their last prayers and embrace each other before being blindfolded and shot.

The chief-of-staff eyed the scene with a mixture of cynicism and admiration. None of them begged or pleaded for their lives with the officer in charge of the firing squad. They accepted death philosophically, even the young ones. The older prisoners even refused the blindfold and shouted 'Long live Poland' as the volley crashed home. He wondered idly if he would be so brave when it came to his turn to be put before some Ivan firing squad, as would undoubtedly be his fate one day soon. He turned away as the officer went down the line of bodies sprawled grotesquely in the dust, blasting away the backs of their skulls, making sure that they were quite dead. Funnily enough that was the part he disliked most. 'The Polacks die bravely,' he remarked casually, as the general stared into nothingness, preoccupied with the new problem that had presented itself in the middle of the planning for the division's new offensive.

'Polacks always die bravely,' he grunted, as if the statement were a matter of fact. 'But what good is dying, bravely or otherwise? Now what do you make of it, Hans? Assuming that the message is reliable and the Ivans have broken through at the God-forsaken village, is it the real thing?'

The chief-of-staff lighted a cigarette and placed it in the ivory cigarette holder which he also affected; it went well with his image of being the division's intellectual — 'the general's grey eminence', as he usually described his role in the mess — when the general was not present. 'I couldn't say, *Standartenführer*. You know the Ivans, they're wily birds. They could be using this breakthrough as a decoy, hoping that we'll send troops up there and then launching the real thing elsewhere. God only knows, they've got enough bodies at their disposal to launch half a dozen decoys!'

Standartenführer Kass nodded his agreement sombrely. He knew that the Russians outnumbered them on this section of the Eastern Front overwhelmingly. Rokossovsky's First Belorussian Army alone had three times the number of effectives of the German 2nd Army, to which his own 5th SS Division was now attached. They could launch heavy probing attacks along the whole front until they found the real weak spot they wanted through which they would pour thousands of T-34s. He bit his bottom lip. 'If we show our hand now, Hans, it might be too premature. All the same, the Führer would have the eggs off both of us with a blunt razor blade if we let the Ivans simply walk through our positions like that!' He snapped his fingers angrily.

Outside another bunch of Polacks were being marched out to the firing range. Before they were shot they had to clear up the mess made by those shot before them; the 5th SS Division was a tidy organization. It liked to do everything in neat German fashion. 'So what do we do?' Instead of answering the *Standartenführer's* question, the chief-of-staff said, 'General, may I give you a brief lecture?'

Kass smiled grimly, showing his gold teeth. 'You usually do, my dear fellow. Proceed.'

'The situation in Eastern Poland at the present time, general, is —'

'A shitty mess.'

'You have a gift of making an apt phrase.'

'*Los, mensch, weiter!*'

'Certainly, sir. Well, the situation is decidedly confused, politically and militarily. The Ivans want the place. We want it and naturally the Polacks want it. But there are two kind of Polacks, red ones, and those who support their exiled government in London.'

'So?'

'So, general, let us do a little playing at God.'

'What do you mean?'

'Let the various factions do the fighting for us. Let the Polacks, Ukrainians and the rest of the mob that are running loose in Eastern Poland take care of this new Ivan drive and move in when it suits us at the least expenditure of German lives.'

The general shook his head. 'I follow you to a certain extent, Hans, but not all the way. Have a little pity on my poor thick head, explain a little more.' He bent his head with both hands in mock anguish.

'All right, sir. The information about the Ivan capture of the village we received from those Ukrainian bandits under the Gorilla: all he wants is for us to tackle them and get our eggs shot off, while he and his merry men do a little looting to the rear where it's nice and safe. We won't do him that favour. Let him harass the Ivans the best he can.'

'But that won't stop the Russian drive?'

'Of course not, sir. But do you think the London Poles and Churchill will clap their hands with joy at the knowledge that the Russians are heading hell-for-leather for the Polish capital?' He answered his own question. 'I doubt it … I doubt it very much. No, Churchill and the rest of those Polacks in London don't want to see all of Poland fall under Russian influence. When we go, they want Poland firmly in Polish hands before the Red Army arrives.'

'When we go?' the general queried without animosity. 'You seem very certain of that fact, *mein Lieber*.'

'We will go, sir. It is as certain as that the sun will ascend into the sky tomorrow morning. We will be lucky if we can manage to hold the eastern border of the Reich itself in a few months' time.'

The general sighed. 'A year ago, Hans, they would have strung you up for even thinking a thought like that.' He shrugged. 'All right, continue.'

'Well, sir, as you know the Gorilla, who gave us the glad news, will cause the Ivans a little trouble, but not much. He won't be able to stop them, that is for certain. But the London Poles could and their Home Army here.'

'But what do they know of the Russian advance?'

'We could tell them,' the chief-of-staff answered simply and beamed at his own cleverness.

'My God,' the general clapped his cropped head again. 'What a crazy world! We stand to one side while armed insurgents, who we are currently shooting out there by the score, are allowed to have a crack at the Ivans. You know, Hans, I do not understand the world anymore. In 1939 I was a simple captain of infantry commanding two hundred big brawny German farm boys. Now I am a divisional commander with fifteen thousand men at my command. But what men? It's like the Foreign Legion out there. I've got frogs, cheeseheads, spaghetti-eaters —I wouldn't be surprised if there weren't a few amis among the ranks of the Fifth! And that is what is called an SS division.' He shook his head sadly. '1944 is a crazy year and 1945 looks as if it's going to be even worse.'

'You want eggs in your beer, general,' Hans answered, understanding the *Standartenführer's* feeling well enough. The times were indeed mad. 'Well, sir, are we going to do it my way?'

'All right, Hans, inform the Polacks through your secret channels. But for God's sake, don't let it get out. The *Reichsheini* would have us shot.' He spoke of Reichsführer SS Heinrich Himmler, head of the SS.

'Never fear, sir,' the chief-of-staff said calmly. 'I want to be alive at the end to see the kind of mess we will be in.'

'You're a cynic, Hans,' the general said, picking up his cap prior to beginning the daily inspection.

'Very likely, sir. It's the only way to stay sane in Poland in this year of Our Lord 1944.'

Outside the shooting of the Poles continued.

The two commanders of the 5th SS Division 'Viking' were not the only ones making plans that morning. Some sixty kilometres away from the German HQ, the colonel of Punishment Battalion 333, his officers, and Major Tennov, commander of the tank battalion, squatted in the dust of the roadside and considered the next move.

The morning was already furnace hot with the broad plain quivering in the blue haze so that the officers had to narrow their eyes against the cutting glare of the sun. During the night they had made excellent progress and were now some dozen kilometres behind the enemy lines without having seen a single German.

'It's almost too good to be true,' Captain Weis commented and watched enviously as a gulag rat, stripped to the waist, plunged his shaven head in a pail of cold water. 'Where have the Fritzes gone to?'

'They're up there ahead somewhere or other,' the colonel replied, taking his eyes off the map spread over his knees. 'They're using their usual tactics.'

'The fortified hedgehog?' Vassily asked.

The colonel nodded. 'Yes, they'll hold the key points, leaving the area between to take care of itself. They can save men like that. The system works to our advantage, as Marshal Rokossovsky anticipated it would. We can slip between the hedgehogs.'

'Not altogether, comrade colonel,' said Tennov, the tank commander, a slight young man with the lobster-red face of a tanker who had been 'flamed' more than once. The words sounded strange and affected as they came from his lipless mouth.

'How do you mean?' the colonel asked, trying not to look too directly at the major's terribly burnt face with its skin drawn tightly over the bones so that it looked like a death's head.

'There's Treblinka up ahead. From the information in my possession, there's no way around it, at least for tanks. *We'll* have to go through the place, unfortunately.'

'Yes, I've already thought about that,' the colonel said. 'According to my calculations we should reach the place just after dusk, which will make our attack easier.'

'For infantry, yes, but definitely not for tanks,' Tennov protested politely but firmly. 'In the dark, a tank is at the mercy of any damn Fritz armed with one of those panzerfausts of theirs. You can get a nasty kick up the arse that way.'

The others laughed, save the colonel. 'That is a risk you will have to take, major. We must reach the Vistula, cost what it may.'

Vassily flashed Vulf a look, but there was no expression save the usual one of intelligent cynicism on the politkommissar's face.

'My plan is as follows,' the colonel went on. 'We'll advance a company of my rats up the road towards Treblinka after dark until they hit opposition. That will be your job, Weis, but you'll avoid getting yourself bogged down in serious trouble. Understood?'

'Understood, comrade colonel,' the dour Volga-German replied, his tone indicating that he did not like the task assigned to him.

'Your first two tanks companies, Major Tennov, with Vassily's rats on the deck, will attack the place on the right and left flank. As soon as you've established yourself in the outskirts of the place, I'll leapfrog my remaining company and the rest of your T-34s through Weis's men in a frontal attack along the road.'

'I don't like it,' Tennov protested, stroking his red boned nose. 'There'll be great losses.'

'You're not supposed to like it,' the colonel replied icily, rising to his feet and packing away his maps. 'Just to carry out orders. It is imperative that we reach the Vistula before the Germans start to reorganize. It will be the only way that our Army can grab Warsaw without a full-scale pitched battle on its hands. Good morning, comrades.'

Hastily the assembled officers sprang to attention, as the colonel stalked away to survey their front.

'*Phew!*' Major Tennov breathed out hard when he had gone. 'I thought you gulag rats were supposed to be battle-shy? Isn't that why they put you in the camps and herd you into battle with the NKVD behind you, armed with machine-guns? But that colonel of yours is a real fire-eater. You'd think he wanted to conquer Eastern Poland single-handed.' He touched his cap and departed back to his tanks, shaking his head like a man sorely tried.

Senior Captain Vassily laughed briefly and said to Vulf. 'Yes, what is getting into the Old Man? Once he thought only of his rats and saving their lives. Now he might well be Old Leather Face in person, sacrificing us all for the greater glory of the Russian Socialist Revolution.'

'*Da, da,*' Captain Weis agreed. 'You've known him longer than any of us, Vulf, what is going on in the colonel's mind?'

Vulf frowned, and stared in bewilderment at the colonel's broad back as he focused his binoculars and stared at the horizon, as if he were wishing the Vistula and Warsaw would appear there in the gleaming circles of calibrated glass. 'If only I knew, comrades. If only I did...' he muttered, almost to himself.

CHAPTER 5

The colonel leaned against the American truck. In fifteen minutes they would be moving on the road march to Treblinka. Now he rested, saving his energy for the battle to come, and listened.

The talk was that of soldiers all over the world: women, food, officers … a combination of the same age-old themes.

'*And the Old Man ain't any better. Look what he did to those poor swine the other day.*'

'*Ay, ay … you're right!*' several voices answered.

'*Out for number one. Gonna buy himself a real regiment at the expense of our lives. After all, we're only miserable gulag rats. What do the likes of us count?*'

The colonel let the words fade away into a distant blur, as he pondered on what he had overheard. Was that what he was really after? Reinstatement and a return to honour in the Red Army, which had been his whole life ever since he had deserted from the Whites to join the Bolsheviks back in 1918?

For nearly two years now since Colonel Katukov, the first commander of the Punishment Battalion had been killed at Stalingrad and he had taken over, he had sought to sublimate himself in the battalion. He had attempted to forget his past, his dead wife, his missing son, his lost rank as marshal of the Soviet Union, even his own name and identity. He had become solely 'the colonel', or as the men knew him behind his back, 'the Old Man': a cold, impersonal figure with no contact with his ever-changing command, save perhaps through that clever little pervert Vulf.

Perhaps the unknown speaker was right. He was trying unconsciously to rehabilitate himself. But for what? For a system that was rotten? To keep Stalin on the throne in the Kremlin? To allow him to fill the camps with ever more gulag rats? No. He remembered the marshal's words and that pronouncement of his: '*One day, little brother, there will be reckoning with that pock-faced swine in the Kremlin.*'

Suddenly everything fell into place and the colonel felt a new purpose surge electrically through his veins. There *was* a reason for capturing Warsaw, whatever the sacrifice in blood and human life. He and those like him *had* to be powerful at the end of the war so that they could wield the muscle necessary to deal with the Georgian tyrant.

As the NCOs' whistles started to shrill, summoning the men to mount up for the new battle, he came round from behind the truck; the men sprang sheepishly and a little fearfully to attention. 'Don't keep scratching your crotch like that, Seminov,' he said to a bearded veteran of the old battalion, who had been busily engaged in rubbing at his flies. 'The crabs have to have lunch too, you know. Save them and pass them on to some nice, plump, juicy Polack pigeon when we get to Warsaw.'

'Yes, Comrade Colonel!' Seminov answered with alacrity, his eyes sparkling as the colonel swept by, a smile on his hard face, knowing that his remark would have passed through the whole battalion by midday...

The Ukrainians took out the petrol trucks just before dusk. They had ascertained that the tanks laden with the infantry intended for the attack on Treblinka were a couple of kilometres ahead of the soft-skinned vehicles and knew they were safe.

The trick they used was as old as the hills, but it worked. Suddenly the first truck driver was confronted by the usual girl MP, posted squarely in the middle of the dusty road, Tommy gun slung over her broad shoulders, little red and black flags at the ready, as if she had been directing traffic there all that long hot July day. He hit the brakes instinctively and the big two-and-half ton American truck came to a halt with a hiss of its air brakes. 'God love a poor lonely soldier,' he gasped to his companion, who had just avoided being thrown through the windscreen. '*Look at those tits!*'

The big blonde MP, whose breasts looked as if they might explode out of her earth-coloured blouse at any moment, advanced sternly towards the column of trucks, flags held up at the stop position.

'ID?' she demanded.

'Holy Mother of God, this is the front!' the driver groaned.

'Think of those beautiful lungs,' his companion whispered. 'Hand it over short, so she'll lean in the cab; I might be able to get a feel.'

But it was more than a feel that the companion got. As the driver leaned out to comply with the female MP's request, a great hairy hand reached in through the open window on the other side and grabbed the companion's throat. He caught one last glimpse of a terrifying hair-covered face dominated by a great black eye-patch; his nostrils were assailed by the fetid stench of rotting teeth, and then the cruel paws were digging into his skinny neck. The petrol convoy had been caught well and truly!

The Gorilla licked his lips and looked at the barrels of fuel that occupied the rear of each truck, while behind him his men killed off the rest of the Russians. 'Must be nearly two hundred of them, perhaps two thousand litres in all,' he calculated slowly, ignoring the screams of pain coming from the dying gulag rats as his men slit their throats. 'Worth a small fortune on the Polack black market.'

With an imperious wave of his hairy black paw he commanded the woman who held up the convoy to come to him. 'Come,' he ordered, 'take them off — and position yourself against that tree.'

The woman flushed with pleasure at being picked out from the half a hundred other women of ten different Slavic nationalities who ran with the band. 'I don't wear them,' she simpered, putting down her Tommy gun and turning round, positioned against the nearest tree.

The Gorilla lifted up her skirt. She had been telling the truth: she was naked beneath it! He admired her plump white buttocks for a moment, then he ripped open his flies and plunged into her expectant body.

Eugen, his second-in-command, who had once in another lifetime been a priest, shook his head at the sight of the chief, as hairy as the animal after which he was nicknamed, copulating with the woman, while around him his men slaughtered the remaining Russian drivers. Life and death in one. They had truly returned to the state of the wild animals.

Once they had been possessed of a high purpose. When the Germans had marched into their native country, they had believed that they would be free again like they had been in 1918. Ukrainians of all shades of opinion had rallied to the crooked-cross flag. In spite of the fact that the Fritzes had behaved with incredible stupidity and cruelty in the Ukraine, they had fought bravely and well for them. But by late 1943 they knew the Fritzes had lost. There would be no free Ukraine. The Russians would be the victors. Then they had become bandits, living off what they could steal during the confused fighting on the Eastern Front, taking their women by force, terrorising, burning, killing, raping — their pure dream of 1941 besmirched, betrayed, dead.

The Gorilla gave one final grunt and, buttoning his flies, slapped the still groaning woman across her buttocks. 'Good,' he said pleased. 'Good. I always like to celebrate a victory with a woman. *Dobre!*'

He turned to Eugen, business-like now. 'All right, clear the road of that Russian scum.'

Eugen rapped out the order to the men, who were busy looting the dead bodies, sprawled everywhere in the dust. A wizened hunchback went from one body to the next, examining their teeth, pincers at the ready to pull out any gold he might find.

'And the petrol? To the Treblinka black market?' Eugen queried.

The Gorilla shook his head. 'Look,' he pointed one heavily ringed finger at the horizon.

Flares were beginning to shoot upwards into the darkening sky and Eugen thought he could make out the faint snap and crack.

'Treblinka,' the Gorilla said, tugging at his eye-patch thoughtfully. 'The Fritzes won't be able to ignore an attack on a place of that size. They'll react now.'

'But those SS swine don't have tanks like the Russians,' Eugen objected.

'And how long, my religious friend, do you think the Russians will be able to keep their battle wagons running, now we've got this?' He jerked a dirty thumb, the size of a small sausage, at the trucks. 'Not long is my guess. Perhaps another fifty kilometres and then they've lost their muscle.'

'And then?' Eugen asked.

'Then we let the Fritzes knock the shit out of them, while we quietly and safely pick up the bits and pieces they leave behind from the dead.'

'Almost as if we were grave robbers,' Eugen whispered, as if he were talking to himself.

'And what did you think we were?' the Gorilla cried and then burst into a tremendous laugh that had something so maniacal about it that it made the small hairs at the back of Eugen's neck stand erect.

CHAPTER 6

Captain Weis crawled down the dry ditch, listening to the howl of the slugs slapping through the bushes above his head and seeing the bright zig-zag of the tracer as it cut through the gloom. He dropped down into the depression next to the foremost rifleman, who fired into the trees to the right of the road with routine precision, as if he were back on some peacetime range.

'What can you see?' he gasped, a little out of breath.

'Not much, comrade captain,' the man replied, not taking his gaze from the trees. 'I think there's a couple of Fritzes in there. They've got either a machine pistol or an automatic. Listen.'

Weis ducked as a burst of tracer ripped above their heads, showering them with a green rain of leaves. 'One of their MG 42s,' he said, identifying the machine-gun. 'They've got a machine-gun nest up there.'

'Could be,' the rifleman answered easily and pumped in another couple of shots.

Weis took a deep breath. He was a brave man, but he didn't like what he was going to be forced to do. At the same time he wondered why he was doing it when half his family had been murdered by the NKVD in 1941 just after the German invasion and the rest of them shipped to the Gulag as potential traitors. It hadn't mattered that his forefathers had lived in Russia since the days of Catherine the Great. Still, the Old Man wanted him to pin down the Germans on the road and pin them down he would.

He rose to his feet, bayonet at the ready, ignoring the tracers hissing towards him from both sides of the road. 'Second

Company!' he bellowed above the angry racket, 'Second Company — *follow me*!'

The gulag rats, fired upon the hundred grammes of vodka which had been handed out just before dusk, came out of their holes with a will, roaring in drunken fury. '*Urrah … urrah*!'

Weis doubled down the road at their head, seeing the scarlet spurts of muzzle flame coming from the trees to left and right. Still no sight of an enemy mortar. They were going to pull it off.

And then they were in among the trees, leaving half a dozen of their comrades sprawled out in grotesque poses on the road behind them. Now it was every man for himself.

A hunched figure started up some fifty metres away from a panting Weis. In spite of the green gloom, he recognized the helmet at once. '*A Fritz*!' he gasped and fired from the hip as he ran. The slug howled off a tree. He had missed the bastard by a dozen metres.

The German whirled and fired his rifle. He, too, missed and then lost his nerve. He dropped his rifle and fell to his knees.

'*Bitte, bitte, Kamerad*!' he cried piteously as Weis raced towards him. '*Nicht schiessen*!'

The words cut Weis to the heart; they were the language of his own people. But he knew the gulag rats could afford to have no mercy.

Crack, crack, crack! the rifle jerked at his hip three times. The man twitched violently each time. Still he didn't go down all the way, swaying there on his knees, thick red blood jetting from his chest.

'*Kamerad* —' Weis caught one last pleading look on that innocent, hairless face and plunged his bayonet home hearing it scrape horribly on the ribcage.

Weis shuddered. The boy's eyes were still open and he made a feeble gesture with one hand. Weis drew the blade out, the steel shining with wet blood and plunged it this time into the soft flesh of the boy's belly. The boy twitched violently as he died, still held upright by the bayonet locked in his guts. Weis could have screamed. He pushed his boot against the sagging body and kicked. Nothing! The boy still hung grimly. He pressed the trigger of his rifle. There was a stench of burning flesh. Blood splattered his uniform. Suddenly the rifle was free.

He staggered against the nearest tree, dimly aware of his men consolidating their positions in the trees, only conscious of the atrocity he had committed. Then the first grunt and howl of a German six-barrel mortar roused him. The Fritzes had bought it! They were going to make a real fight for the road. Perhaps their reserves were already rushing from Treblinka to come to the aid of the defenders? Sobbing for breath, his shoulders heaving, as if he had just run a great race, Weis pulled out the signal pistol. With an unsteady hand he fired two green flares. They hissed into the sky colouring all below a sickly unnatural hue. It was the signal.

'The flares — two green, comrade colonel!' Vulf snapped.

The colonel embraced Vassily in the Russian fashion, bussing him on both cheeks and shook hands hastily with a still resentful Tennov.

Tennov sprang up on to the turret of the lead T-34, followed an instant later by Captain Vassily.

Tennov shouted something. His driver hit the accelerator. A cloud of blue smoke streamed from the T-34's exhausts. Tennov raised his signal flags. Behind him engine after engine burst into noisy life. The evening air was full of the acrid stench of fuel.

Vassily looked down at the colonel and shouted something above the racket.

The colonel couldn't hear.

Vassily held up his right hand in the symbol of a Roman gladiator about to enter the arena to fight and die.

The colonel shook his head, a weary little smile on his sad lips, as if to say, 'No, little brother, not this time — and not you.'

Then with a shower of earth from its tracks, the command tank lurched forward, followed by T-34 after T-34, each one's decks packed with gulag rats, crouched down behind the turrets, weapons clutched in sweaty hands as the tanks burst through the hedges and started to left and right, heading for a Treblinka which was already beginning to burn for a reason still unknown to the colonel.

Punishment Battalion 333 was going in for the big attack.

The thick blob of white came racing at the lead tank, gathering speed at every moment. 'Hold tight,' Tennov gasped, 'solid shot AP.'

'What are we supposed to do?' Vassily yelled above the roar of the T-34's engines, as the anti-tank shell came roaring ever closer.

'Well, if I weren't an atheist, I'd say pray,' Tennov roared and ducked behind the protection of the turret.

Hastily Vassily did the same.

Next instant the six-pound shell hit the side of the turret with a great ringing blow. The whole thirty-four ton tank trembled. Below the driver gasped with shock. Vassily could not. His horrified gaze was fixed on the side of the turret. It glowed a dull, frightening red, as the shell traced its way along the outside. Tennov gulped. 'If it penetrates, this place will be full of flying shit,' he explained in a weak voice. 'I've seen it before. AP doesn't stop till it takes the turnip off'n every shitting one of us!'

The couple of seconds seemed to take an eternity. Then as suddenly as it had come, the red glow inside the turret vanished, though Vassily could still feel the terrific heat, and the anti-tank shell whizzed off harmlessly into space.

Tennov spun the periscope. 'Gunner!'

'Comrade major.'

'Fritz gun — two o'clock!' He rapped out the order before Vassily had recovered. 'Three hundred metres — *Fire*!'

Frantically the sweating gunner at their side carried out the officer's orders. He tugged at the firing bar. The tank trembled and reared up on its front bogies. Thick, acrid smoke invaded the turret. Hastily Tennov pressed the smoke extractor, automatically opening his mouth so that his ear drums wouldn't burst. The breech rattled open and a gleaming smoking brass shell-case tumbled to the metal floor in the same instant that the next German shell howled just above the turret.

'God in heaven!' Vassily cursed, dark eyes wide with fear, 'and I thought the gulag rats lived dangerously! Why, these tin cans are nothing better than mobile coffins.'

Tennov smiled thinly and rapped, 'Gunner, lower it fifty metres. You're overshooting!'

There was a great, booming, hollow sound as a shell struck the T-34's chassis. The tank trembled violently, as if caught by a huge wind.

For a moment Vassily thought all was finished. The motors did not seem to be turning over and the turret was filled with the stink of fumes, as if a battery or fuel tank had been hit.

Then they were moving again and the gunner was roaring, 'Got the Fritz bastard! *Got him!*'

A dazed, frightened gulag rat risked a quick look over the edge of the turret. A couple of hundred metres to their right, an anti-tank gun blazed, its gunners sprawled around it like bundles of torn rags, its barrel peeled like a banana skin.

But already there were new dangers coming their way: low lean half-tracks, their machine guns spitting fire as they raced at a tremendous speed over the rough fields towards the T-34s.

'Bazooka men,' Tennov yelled hastily. 'The brave bastards!'

'Why?' Vassily asked somewhat foolishly.

But Tennov did not need to answer the question for him; he could see what was happening with his own eyes. The half-tracks tearing around in a great wake of dust were discharging little figures from their rears, who were running frantically for cover, lugging their heavy awkward panzerfausts with them.

Tennov dug the gunner violently in the ribs. 'HE and machine-gun fire, you great oaf!' he bellowed and grabbing the second turret machine-gun himself, directed a wild burst of curving white tracer at the running Germans.

Vassily didn't like it one bit, but he knew it had to be done. The tankers couldn't handle the bazooka men in the dark by themselves. He swung himself out of the turret, before Tennov could stop and bellowed above the roar of the engine and the chatter of the machine-guns, 'Gulag rats, follow me!' He aimed a kick at the nearest rat and the man dropped over the side, enclosed immediately by the great cloud of dust being flung up by the flailing tracks, as the driver zig-zagged instinctively knowing the danger the tank faced in the darkness. Man after man followed.

'Form a skirmish line!' he screamed as the tanks raced by the men forming up in the thick clouds of dust. 'Skirmish line, I said —'

There was a light dry crack. Scarlet flame stabbed the gloom. A great dark clumsy object hurtled towards the nearest tank, trailing angry red sparks behind it. Vassily ducked instinctively. There was the sound of a great hammer descending upon a mighty anvil. The tank staggered to a halt, as if it had just run into a brick wall. Next instant the night was torn apart by a great white sheet of blinding light.

'By the great whore!' Vassily cursed, as the ten-ton turret of the stricken T-34 sailed majestically through the air, and thudded down shaking the very earth some dozen metres away.

Almost immediately another rocket struck another tank and turned it into a great ball of fire, with human torches staggering away from it.

Vassily could well imagine what Major Tennov was thinking at this moment, as yet another of his beloved T-34s was hit, coming to a slow stop, its track unrolling behind it like a severed limb. His worst fears of using tanks in a semi-built up area in the dark were being realized.

And then they were charging the bazooka men, their bayonets glinting in the ruddy light of the burning tanks, mad yells rising from their parched, wide-opened mouths, teeth bared wolfishly. The opposing lines buckled under the impact and suddenly the night air was full of the blood-chilling shrieks of crazed men locked in combat.

They hacked, slashed, gouged, stabbed, flesh pounding flesh, the men screaming, sobbing, sweating with fear, ploughing each other into the ground.

The Germans had had enough. They broke. Screaming and tearing each other, throwing away their weapons in their haste to get away from the gulag rats, one last German following the rest, legs spread absurdly wide apart, dragging his entrails behind him, calling piteously for his comrades to wait for him until, pitching over on his own guts, he was finished off with a burst of Vassily's Tommy gun.

Two red signal flares hissed into the burning sky over Treblinka. Now the final attack could go in.

The colonel led the drive into the Polish town himself. Vicious purple tongues of flame leapt up from the low buildings on all sides. A couple of horses, broken out of some stable, manes and tails blazing a fierce red, galloped panic-stricken down the body-littered street.

Behind the colonel's lead tank a T-34 was hit and smashed completely out of control into a small house. Masonry tumbled down, burying it. The colonel's gunner sprayed the building to the right. Even above the rattle of the tracks they heard the scream of the bazooka man as he fell from the upper window and smashed to the cobbles below. In the next instant the tracks rolled over him pressing him into the road like a blood-red cardboard figure.

But now the backbone was going out of the German resistance. They were already withdrawing from the burning town. As the lead tank swung by the little station, the Poles, mostly women, were busy looting the *Wehrmacht* food train, fighting and screaming hysterically at each other in their desire for the precious tinned goods, trampling over the pulped body of the elderly guard who had tried to stop their rush. Everywhere there were Poles looting whatever they could find, useful and useless, dragging away their booty in handcarts or pushing it in wheel-barrows, ignoring the murder and mayhem on all sides and the tracer zipping back and forth through the glowing darkness.

The lead tank swung out of the main square, the gunner spraying both sides of the street with slugs, the bullets pocking the brick wall with jagged holes, while the enemy bullets howled harmlessly off their steel sides.

To their left lay a long line of dead and dying horses, still in their traces, harnessed to a column of abandoned German Army wagons, their skinny ribs showing through their moth-eaten coats. Already Polish housewives, armed with knives and kitchen-pails, were appearing from everywhere and beginning to carve up the dying horses, their hands red with blood to the wrists, desperate to get a share of the precious meat before it was all gone.

The colonel swallowed back the bitter bile which threatened to choke him. In his long career of war in two continents he had seen some terrible things, but nothing like this night-time capture of Treblinka. In war he expected soldiers to go slightly mad — who wouldn't in view of what they had to suffer on the battlefield? — but here the whole world seemed to have gone crazy. If there were a real hell, then it was in Treblinka this night.

But there was worse to come before dawn lit the little Polish town with its first ugly white light.

CHAPTER 7

It was the appalling stench which caught the colonel's attention.

It was like nothing he had ever smelled before: a thick cloying stink, composed of human sweat, infinite human misery and charred human flesh. The only comparison he could make was that it seemed a little like the rancid, penetrating stench he had once experienced in the monkey house of a provincial zoo as a boy: something he had not been able to ban from his nostrils for many a day, in spite of the handkerchief, soaked in cheap cologne, that he had kept pressed to his nose.

Then the tank swung round the corner and he saw where it was coming from.

A camp! A camp like so many that had spread loathsomely across Europe from the Urals to the Channel in these last awful years: a great hexagon of faeces-littered earth, surrounded by triple barriers of barbed wire, now torn down in many places. But now the machine-guns which had once guarded the inmates were gone and the men who had manned them trampled to death, beaten into the very earth by the thousands and ever more thousands of walking skeletons clad in what looked like striped pyjamas. They streamed out of the gates, many of them falling never to rise again, hands stretched out to grab the Red Army, screaming a hysterical 'welcome' in a dozen European languages.

Next to the colonel, the sergeant tank commander crossed himself rapidly, as if the devil himself was descending upon him and below the driver gasped, '*boshe moi*... What are they, in God's name, what are they, comrade colonel?'

The colonel knew well enough what they were, these grotesque creatures with their great gleaming eyes that bulged from emaciated faces, the cheekbones enormous and abnormally large, their arms and legs mere bones clad in skin, great wreaths of withered tissue hanging around their genitals, their shaven skulls gory, red and dripping with hideous sores. It was the gulag all over again, but a gulag more terrifying and murderous than any he had ever encountered in the years in Stalin's camps. 'Halt ... halt the tank,' he gulped, as they staggered, limped, crawled straight towards its whirling tracks. 'For God's sake, man, hit the brakes!'

'*Mangez!*'

'*Mangare!*'

'*Essen!*'

'*Voda ... kleba...*'

The pitiful cries came from all sides and hundreds of skinny arms, running with lice, the fingers crusted with scabies reached up pleadingly for food, while those too weak to cry squatted in the faeces of the yard and stared up at him with those terrible gleaming eyes.

The colonel swallowed and tried to control himself.

'*Ponemayvtiapa russki?*' he demanded of an old man with a thin white beard and still intelligent eyes who had crowded to the front of the wildly excited crowd.

'*Da da, ya ponemayu pa russki,*' the old man croaked in a thick accent, which the colonel couldn't identify. 'What is this place, old man?'

'Treblinka camp, *tovaritisch pan,*' the old man quavered. He waved his hand at the still smoking chimneys behind him. 'Do you not see the ovens?'

'But what has happened here?' the colonel demanded, catching out of the corner of his eyes ever more people crowding around the tank and wondering how long it would be before they would be swarming all over it in their desperate search for food.

'They bring us here. They make us work. When we no longer can work they put us in the ovens and we go up like this,' he raised one skinny forefinger and made the sign of smoke ascending into the sky.

The colonel could guess who the 'they' were — the Fritzes.

'And what happened just now?'

The old man took off his striped cap and held it in front of his chest in the old-fashioned way of a *moujik*, a peasant greeting his lord. 'If it pleases you, *pan*, when we heard the tanks, we knew we were saved. We broke down the wire. Oh, they shot us by the dozen, but we broke it down and we were free.'

'Yes, we killed the swine, did for them for good,' another voice added in Polish-accented Russian.

'*Palshalsze*, *pan*,' the old man concluded humbly, 'give us food, *voda kleba* ... we are dying.' He pointed to what was a mockery of a human child sucking at the long, wrinkled, empty dug of the skeletal woman standing next to him. '*Moloka* for the children.' The colonel had never been confronted with a situation like this before. '*We die ... we die...*' he sobbed, thick grey tears rolling down his sunken cheeks.

The colonel shouted for order, but they were too excited to hear. He saw they were getting completely out of hand. Grabbing the turret machine-gun, he fired a quick burst into the air.

The noise died down almost immediately and he bellowed in Russian. 'I will see what I can do! But we are fighting soldiers behind the German lines. We carry little food.'

'But you will try, *tovaritisch pan*?' the old man quavered.

'I will try.' The colonel gave the tank commander a quick dig in the ribs. 'Let's get the hell out of here while the going's good, sergeant. Move it!'

He moved it.

It was dawn. The fires were beginning to burn down in Treblinka, filling the air with the dirty stink of burnt cloth and timber. Now the Poles had barricaded themselves back into their houses, their food secure, oblivious to the pyjama-clad skeletons wandering aimlessly through the body-littered streets on tottering pipe-stem legs, looking for scraps, searching the corpses for food, sucking at the raw bones they had torn from the horses.

'What are we going to do about them, Colonel?' Vassily asked as the senior officers squatted in the lee of a tank, drinking green tea.

The colonel looked around the circle of their young faces, each one blanched, anxious, shocked — hard as they all were — by what they had seen that morning. Tennov even had tears in his eyes, but then obviously he had never seen the gulag. 'What exactly do you expect me to do, comrades?' he asked mildly.

'But we are all gulag rats,' Weis protested. 'We have all experienced the camps. We have seen injustice and starvation enough. Though they might even be Jews up there,' he flung an angry gesture in the direction of the concentration camp, 'we are all brothers, brothers in suffering, comrade colonel.'

'The heart has its reasons, colonel,' Vulf said softly, studying the colonel's harsh tormented face, 'for which there is no understanding in the brain. It tells us that we owe a debt to those who are the same kind of — er — scum as ourselves.'

'Agreed,' Vassily and half a dozen of the others said quickly. 'We can't let them just die like that. We must get help, most of all, *food*.'

The colonel thought for a while. 'If we bog down here, the Fritzes might well counter-attack and then —,' he shrugged and did not finish his sentence.

But they understood what he meant. That might mean the end of their dash for the Vistula.

'All it would mean is that we contact the point of the follow-up, Colonel,' Vassily said hastily. 'Perhaps ten ... twelve hours at the most and in the meantime give those poor creatures our rations, whatever we can find here in the town, the German food dumps haven't all been looted and we could force the Poles to give up some of the stuff they've stolen. Colonel,' he said, leaning forward, his handsome face strained and tense, 'half a day, that is all. But it might mean the difference between life and death for that,' he flung out his hand and indicated a pathetic half-naked creature with a monstrous bulbous head, sitting in the gutter carefully picking the hayseed out of a horse apple.

The colonel nodded. 'All right, I shall contact the marshal himself on the radio and explain the situation.' He glanced around the circle of relieved faces. 'But remember this, comrades, we abide by his decision. There will be no further discussion whatever it may be.' And with that he was gone.

The marshal listened to what he had to say without any interruption and, in spite of the static caused by the many Red

Army units grouped around his HQ on the Russian-Polish border, the colonel sensed that he was thinking hard as he listened. Finally the colonel was finished and rasped 'over'.

The marshal did not reply immediately, but kept the colonel waiting. When he did speak, his words were firm and determined and the listening man knew he would not change his mind; it was made up.

'I understand well your position, little brother. After all I was a gulag rat myself once. But let me quote you something I once heard from the mouth of Old Leather Face himself. "The death of one man is a tragedy. The death of a million men is a mere statistic." Those unfortunate people in that camp of yours will go in to history as a statistic, that is, if the fact is ever recorded in history.' The listening man caught a trace of bitterness in the marshal's voice. 'No, you will continue your drive with all possible speed. When we reach Treblinka we will do what we can do. That is all, colonel. Over.' He ended, his voice quite neutral, although he knew and the colonel knew that he had just condemned hundreds, perhaps, thousands of innocent people to their death; 'over and out'. □

The colonel walked back slowly to the waiting officers.

'Well?' Weis, unable to contain himself any longer, blurted out.

Vulf already knew the marshal's decision; he could see it written all over the Old Man's face. Still he waited tensely like the rest.

'We march,' the colonel answered coldly, 'on the hour. We continue the drive for the Vistula. The marshal has ordered we are not to stop here in Treblinka.'

There were mumbles of protests from the others. Vulf watched the Old Man's face and could tell by the twitching of the jaw muscles that he was fighting some inner conflict. But what was it? Why was it so important for a gulag rat to get to the Vistula? Why was the Old Man fighting for the greater glory of Old Leather Face who had once condemned them all to the misery of the camps, just like the Fritzes had condemned those poor wretches up the road to their camp?

'And what about the point of the follow-up force then?' Vassily asked.

'Oh, yes, that is another thing. The marshal informed me the road behind us has been cut — mines apparently. He thinks it's those Ukrainian renegades I told you about at the briefing.' He looked directly at Major Tennov. 'They've got your fuel too. The whole shitting lot.'

'But that means my tanks'll run out of juice in about...' a confused, angry Tennov made a hurried calculation, 'in say thirty kilometres. What are we gonna do then?'

The colonel gave him a cold, bitter smile. 'Major, then you'll do what the gulag rats have always done. *You'll march or croak...*'

CHAPTER 8

The general, now known as 'Bor', walked down the hot Warsaw street in the July sunshine, dressed in a shabby raincoat, a large felt hat pulled down over his high forehead. Thin, balding, thoughtful looking, his face with its small clipped military moustache, set in its usual melancholic expression, he looked like so many other Poles who had been beaten and oppressed these last five years.

He entered Pavia Street and started walking to the Kemmler Factory, which housed the secret headquarters; humbly he took his hands out of his pockets as a sign of respect for the bored German sentry, standing behind his machine-gun, which rested on a pile of sandbags. If the sentry noticed the gesture, he gave no sign of doing so; the Germans expected the Poles to act humbly in their presence. After all they were the conquerors.

Bor approached the brown building, which before Poland's defeat in the autumn of 1939 had been a tobacco factory. Carefully he looked to left and right. After all, the quarter swarmed with Germans. But there were none in sight. He knocked three times and was admitted immediately.

All the leaders of the *Armja Krajowa*, the Home Army, were present in the upper room, where they had been meeting now for the last week — ever since they had decided that the uprising must take place soon or never.

Bor nodded his greeting and got down to business at once in his usual impatient manner... 'Gentlemen, I have been informed that the Reds — er excuse me, the Russians — have reached Treblinka.'

Some of the officers smiled at his slip. Most of them fought the Russians back in 1920 and a few of them once more in 1939 when they had joined Hitler to divide Poland between Russia and Germany. Officially now the Russians were allies — privately they were the hated Reds.

'So what do we do about them?' Bor answered his own question. 'There are two possibilities. We can help them to get to the capital as quickly as possible and then start our uprising against the Germans. Or...' He raised his finger in warning, knowing specifically the dangers the second alternative presented. 'We can hinder their progress until the uprising is well and truly underway and the capital is in our hands — *Polish hands!*' He paused and let the words sink in.

Brigadier Okulicki, the hard, professional soldier who had recently been parachuted into Poland as the representative of the Polish Exile Government in London, was the first off the mark. 'I vote we fight now,' he said in his ebullient, impetuous manner. 'The Germans are collapsing. They have been passing troops through Warsaw for days now, and, gentlemen, I know a beaten army when I see one.'

Some of the others nodded their agreement. The brigadier had played an important part in defending Warsaw in September 1939; he had been a commander of a defeated army then. He knew.

'Even with the forces at our disposal, as poorly trained and armed as they are, I think we can take and hold Warsaw against whatever the Fritzes care to throw against us.'

'Remember last year when the ghetto revolted against them?' someone objected.

Okulicki shrugged carelessly. 'Jews,' he said. 'In two thousand years of existence they have never fought for their freedom. We are Poles. We have always fought for ours.'

There was a mumble of agreement from the others.

Bor sucked his overlarge front teeth thoughtfully, while they waited. 'You understand,' he said finally, 'that we will have to rely entirely upon our own resources? Perhaps a few weapons flown in from Italy and dropped by parachute, and if our people in London can convince Churchill, with luck the Polish Parachute Brigade in that country. It is a risk.'

'It is a risk we have to take for Poland,' Brigadier Okulicki snapped, his dark eyes blazing. 'The Fritzes are running away. Before the Reds arrive, we must have Warsaw in our hands.' He raised his broad peasant paws, as if he were bearing the whole weight of the capital in them. 'There is no other way that we can deal with that monster in the Kremlin. *Fait accompli*, gentlemen, that is all he understands.'

Bor sighed. 'All right, so be it, gentlemen. From now onwards the Home Army in Warsaw is on a twenty-four hour alert notice.'

There was a collective sigh of relief from the brigadier and his followers. 'Now what are we going to do about those Reds heading for the Vistula?' Okulicki followed up quickly.

Bor frowned. It was bad enough that they were soon going to tackle the German Army, beaten though it might be, with a handful of trained soldiers and a mass of untrained civilians. Now the new situation entailed them taking on the Red Army as well. 'I have thought about it,' he said slowly. 'Of course, we cannot undertake any large scale operations against the — oh, damn it — the Reds!'

The others grinned.

'As I see it, though, our comrades on the other side of the river might put certain obstacles in the way of our new-found allies from the east, though naturally those allies do not need to know that it is the Home Army which is putting those obstacles in their way.'

'Exactly,' the brigadier snapped. 'Eastern Poland is a sewer. Who can tell who is fighting who?' ☐

Bor nodded his agreement.

'So what have you got in mind for them?'

Bor frowned at Okulicki and asked himself why the man must always be so damn direct. There was not one bit of subtlety in the man's whole body. 'As far as I can gather the Reds are advancing in a small battle group of tanks and infantry, perhaps some two thousand men at the most. Not a particularly large force, though of course I wouldn't let one of our units tackle them in open combat in the field. That would never do.'

'Of course not,' Okulicki snapped. 'But there are other ways?'

'Yes. Assuming that they are advancing from Treblinka towards the Vistula heading for — say — Praga, they must take second-class roads to avoid the German hedgehogs, keeping the River Bug to their right to protect that flank, at least against any kind of German counter-attack. So we ascertain the particular road or roads they are going to use and block them. There is no need for an open fight.'

'Agreed,' Okulicki snapped once again with that brutal directness of his. 'Mines, anti-personnel and anti-tank, on the road and to a depth of half a kilometre on both sides, covered by — say — a couple of companies, dressed in German uniform, just in case they have to tackle the Reds.'

What a boor, Bor told himself. The man made no pretensions whatsoever to military etiquette. He said the first thing that came to his mind. Admittedly though, he was right: that was the way it should be done. 'And who do you suggest, brigadier, should be given the task?' There was heavy irony in his voice. After all he knew better than Okulicki who was available. But irony was wasted on the representative of the Exile Government. 'Snot-Face and the German,' he said immediately, using the nickname of two of the Home Army's commanders in Eastern Poland.

Custom demanded the two leaders should be referred to by their code-names as Bor was instead of his real name of Tadeusz Komorowski. But evidently Okulicki completely ignored such things. He blurted out their nicknames, which could well give away their true identities in other circumstances. 'Snot-Face' was a former officer who had been hit in the face in the September fighting. Since then his sinus had given him trouble and he was always dripping mucus disgustingly from his red, swollen nose — hence the nickname. 'The German's' identity could soon be discovered from his nickname. There weren't many ethnic Germans serving in the ranks of the Home Army. Most of them had run over to the Fritzes as soon as they had invaded Poland in 1939.

'So be it,' Bor contented himself with saying. 'They will hold up the Reds.'

'How long?' someone asked.

'I would think perhaps … forty-eight hours,' Bor said slowly.

Okulicki flashed him an excited look. 'You mean you have made up your mind, Bor?'

Bor's face showed no such animation. He knew what the brigadier thought of him. He regarded Bor as a stick-in-the-mud, who was always hesitating to take bold action, but then the brigadier did not have to concern himself with the fates of thousands of Poles who had fought underground for five years, with the fate of Poland itself. Under such circumstances one did not make decisions quickly or lightly.

'Not quite, brigadier. I don't think the time is far off when we must revolt against the Germans, but I have not yet decided when that hour will be. For the present we will remain by our decision to place the Home Army on a twenty-four hours' alert notice.'

Okulicki snorted angrily, but said nothing. Thus the vital meeting came to an end without a final decision about when the rising should start.

But far away from the tobacco factory, Stalin, that same morning, made a decision which would force Bor's hand.

Sitting in his throne-like chair in the Kremlin, a glass of his favourite pepper vodka in one hand in spite of the early hour, curved pipe in the other, his swarthy, pockmarked face set in thought, the Soviet dictator pondered the events in Poland.

One by one the countries of Eastern Europe were falling into his hands and he wanted Poland too, just as the czars who had occupied this same palace had wanted it, hungrily, avidly, like an old man might lust for a young juicy, mistress. He knew of course, that neither that American fool Roosevelt, nor even that drunken old fox Churchill, would ask him to give Eastern Poland back to the Poles. What he had taken in 1939, he would keep. He knew it and they did too.

But Western Poland and Warsaw were a different thing. Churchill would insist that the London Exile Government be allowed to have that part of the war-torn country at least. And Roosevelt would be too scared of losing the Polish vote in Chicago, Pittsburgh and those other Polish cities the next time they played that silly democrat game of theirs. But what if there were no Polish resistance to come back to? What if the Exile Government flew in from London to a Poland firmly under Red Army control with his own Polacks of the Lublin

Government running a puppet regime? What could they do then?

Stalin puffed out a cloud of smoke which he followed with his dark, cunning eyes as it drifted upwards to the ornate ceiling while his aides and advisers watched him in awed silence, wondering what was going on in his brain.

'*Nothing!*' Stalin told himself. 'Absolutely nothing.'

In essence, he thought, it was all a question of timing. He knew from his agents inside the Polish capital that the Polacks who served London were about to rise. He knew too from similar sources that the Germans were not as beaten as the Poles suspected. If the Poles could be persuaded to rise now, the Germans might well massacre them for him; and the capital would be his for the taking. Then Churchill and that bunch of Polacks in London would be without a country to govern.

He crooked his finger at his secretary.

Aleksander Poskrebyshev, hunchback, undersized, sinister, limped towards his master, a suitable secretary for the monster. 'Yes, comrade?' the secretary said in his unctuous voice, rubbing his hands, as if they were very cold in spite of the heat of the morning. 'You wish?'

'This, comrade,' The two of them were exceedingly polite with each other, almost formal, as if both recognized in each other the sadist, the plotter, the murderer. 'I want you to have Radio Moscow broadcast a statement in Polish.'

The secretary produced a pencil and paper as if by magic from his shabby jacket and waited attentively.

Stalin raised his eyes to the ceiling and started to compose the message aloud, 'For Warsaw ... which never capitulated ... and never gave up the struggle ... the hour of action has struck.'

The secretary risked a glance from his pad, dark eyes full of admiration for his master's cunning. He could guess what the old fox was up to.

'By fighting ... in the streets of Warsaw, in the houses, factories and stores ... we shall bring nearer the moment of ultimate liberation and we shall preserve the country's wealth and the lives of our brothers.'

Even as he wrote, the hunchback could guess what Stalin was about. The message would convince the Polacks that the Red Army was in trouble, and that it needed the extra help a rising in the capital would give it. The Polacks would think that now was the most opportune time to clear out the Fritzes before the Red Army could drive to the capital. They would rise. But what they didn't know was that the Fritzes were ready to wipe them off the face of the earth.

He risked a little smile at the dictator sitting there in his throne, sucking at his big working man's pipe, looking with his flowing dyed moustache, like some old *kulak* who had just cheated his neighbour of a juicy little piglet.

Stalin smiled back, but there was no warmth in those dark, brooding eyes of his, just death...

CHAPTER 9

The Snot-Face, a heavy brute of a man, hated by the enemy, his friends, even his own company which profited most by his high-handed manner, dragged the ancient headman out of his hut by his ear and said, 'This day we stop the Reds. I want all your villagers, men, women and children to help us to lay those.' He indicated the bullock-drawn carts, heaped high with turnips under which lay the looted German mines.

'But *pan*,' the skinny old man quavered, 'the Russians, they will slaughter us once they find out we have helped. I have known the Russians since the day of Alexander the Second, they are a ruthless people.'

Snot-Face guffawed and closing his good nostril, snorted and showered the earth with a great gob of opaque snot. 'We are more ruthless, old one. We must all make sacrifices.'

'They will burn the village.'

'So,' Snot-Face smashed his fist into the old man's face. Blood poured from his broken lips and two yellow teeth dropped on to his beard. 'I will burn the village — and shoot you as well.'

'We will do as you say, sir,' the old man said thickly through a mouthful of warm, salty blood.

'I thought you would,' Snot-Face said easily. 'Give me something to eat.' He pointed to the smoked ham hanging from the rafters of the headman's hut. 'That, and some vodka for my men.'

'Certainly, *pan*,' the old man said hastily and handed him the ham.

Snot-Face drew his razor-sharp knife and cut himself a large slice of the excellent air-dried ham, which had been rubbed well with garlic, black pepper and alcohol. He swallowed, head upraised, Adam's apple going up and down like a lift, as a stork swallows a frog.

While the peasants went to work, digging in the mines on both sides of the road, the men of the Home Army passed the bottles of potato vodka, illegally brewed in the miserable village, from hand to hand and watched, listening to Snot-Face lecture them. 'The whip is all those peasant swine understand,' he rambled on, taking great sniffs in an attempt to clear his right nostril, but in vain. 'They only help us when they are afraid. Poland's fate does not concern them one little turd. For us there is only victory or death. Our lives are worth nothing. But for them life is everything. For them there is always a planting and a harvest.'

For those among his listeners who were educated and could think, it was not difficult to realize that these last terrible years in the underground had turned Snot-Face slightly mad. Others among them shivered, in spite of the morning heat, and directed their attention to the potato vodka. A few realized that Okulicki in Warsaw had picked the ideal man for the job on hand. Snot-Face was too crazy to know what fear was. He was an Ascension Day candidate *par excellence*...

The peasants finished and the headman stood there, the dry blood turning black and hard at the corner of his mouth, ragged cap in hand saying humbly. 'Now what, *pan*?'

'This! Burn this pigsty of a village of yours to attract the Reds' attention — they would do it anyway — and then get out before I change my mind and fry you with it.'

Half an hour later the little village was ablaze and Snot-Face's men were dug in on both sides of the road, waiting. They would not wait long.

Tennov's tankers were using standard operating procedure for a reconnaissance operation. A T-34 crawled slowly down the empty road, gun twitching from side to side like the snout of some predatory monster searching out its prey, while half a kilometre behind it another T-34 followed its progress, ready to report back if the first tank ran into trouble. Contact between the two tanks was minimal, maintained by flag signals; unlike the *Wehrmacht*, radio contact did not exist in the Red Army's tank corps.

For some ten minutes now the attention of the commander in the first tank had been held by the sight of the burning village to his right front. He had come to the conclusion that the Fritzes had set it on fire and they had done so because they were retreating. Otherwise they would not have destroyed houses which would have given them shelter and protection. Perhaps because of that, he did not pay sufficient attention to the road and note the tell-tale marks on it that would have normally indicated to him that there were mines. He was to pay for that oversight with his life.

The T-34 lurched over the first lump. Nothing happened. It was one of the anti-personnel mines that Snot-Face's men had planted there. The second mine was an anti-tank mine, a stolen German teller-mine. There was a soft rumble as the mine started to explode. Suddenly the tank heaved. Its tracks snapped and rolled away. A bogie flew off. Slowly, very slowly, the tank rose into the air and landed with a great crash in the field to the left. Nobody got out.

Five hundred metres behind it, the second tank came to an abrupt stop. For a long moment, its commander waited. Nothing stirred to his front. Then he snapped an order to the gunner. The turret swung round slowly, cranked as it was by hand, until the 75mm long-barrelled cannon pointed at the burning village. 'Fire!' the commander ordered.

Flame stabbed from the muzzle. The tank trembled and a high explosive shell hurtled towards the village. It exploded, throwing up burning debris and earth. Still nothing happened. The tank commander did not like the situation he found himself in. He needed the protection of infantry. He gave the driver an order. The driver needed no urging. They were like a sitting duck, high on the road like this and stationary as well. He thrust the big gear into reverse and the T-34 backed down the road, its long cannon swinging from side to side protectively until they were round the bend and out of sight of anyone who might be lurking out there to the front.

Five minutes later the gulag rats were on their way. They came level with the still smoking crater where the mine had been planted and broke into two groups, moving left and right into the fields. They ran into trouble almost at once.

The leading sergeant, one of those who had manned the machine-guns when they had shot the gulag rats against the wall, felt the metal object beneath his foot and knew instinctively he had stepped on a mine. But by then it was too late. The murderous device exploded with a dry crack like a twig underfoot. The sergeant screamed. Slowly he began to fall, his head whirling, thick red blood gushing from his crotch.

Then there were screams everywhere as man after man went down. The minefield had done its work...

'Shit,' the colonel said, as they pulled the last screaming victim out by means of a rope tied round his chest. 'What a goddam shitting mess!' Automatically he ducked as the sniper covering the minefield fired and the slug whined off a tree only half a dozen metres away.

'What now?' Tennov asked, eyeing his shattered tank miserably. Now they had fuel for perhaps ten more kilometres at the most.

'We've got to get through it,' the colonel answered, glancing at the terrain.

'But how?'

'We could use your tanks, Tennov?'

The major looked at him aghast. 'Those mines would slaughter us.'

'I've heard there is a little trick of reinforcing the tank bottom with sandbags to give extra protection,' the colonel continued half-heartedly. 'That might get your T-34s through, Tennov.'

The major shook his head firmly. 'I'm not going to risk any more of my tanks that way, colonel, not to mention my men. The sandbags wouldn't help much.'

'I suppose you're right, Tennov,' the colonel said, dismissing the thought. He hadn't held out much hope for it as it was. In his heart he knew there was only one way of getting through that minefield. He took Tennov by the arm. 'Have you still got any smoke shells left?'

Somewhat mystified by the sudden change of direction in the conversation, the major nodded.

'And do you think you could lay some sort of smoke screen around that wood to the right?'

'I suppose, I could.'

'For how long?'

Tennov made a quick calculation. 'Half an hour at the most,' he announced.

'It'll have to do.' The colonel turned to Vassily. 'What's our chance of getting a couple of volunteers from the rats?'

Vassily, half guessing what the colonel was going to do, laughed scornfully. 'Gulag rats don't volunteer, comrade colonel. You should know that.' He clicked to attention. 'One volunteer present and ready, colonel!'

The colonel laughed too and pressed his arm affectionately. 'Good for you, Vassily.'

'You're going to clear a path through the field under cover of smoke, aren't you, colonel?'

The colonel nodded, the smile gone from his somewhat bitter mouth. 'Yes, if we can clear a path wide enough for one tank with infantry support, I think that should do it. My guess is there's not much more than a company of Fritz infantry over there.'

Vassily nodded his agreement.

'Once they see the T-34, they'll hoof it. Infantry usually does, even Fritz infantry.'

Vassily again nodded his agreement. 'When?' he asked simply.

'As soon as it's dark.'

Vassily whistled softly. 'Clear a minefield in the dark, colonel,' he exclaimed. 'Couldn't you make it a little harder — like doing it blindfolded?'

CHAPTER 10

Now it was silent, save the persistent, maddening chirping of the crickets. The wood where the enemy was hidden was shrouded in the growing gloom, devoid of any sign of life. All the same the colonel and Vassily knew the Germans hadn't pulled out. They were there all right — and alert, too.

The colonel pulled the long bayonet out of his belt. Reluctantly Vassily did the same. Tennov nodded he was ready and his lips formed the words 'good luck'.

Vassily gave him a sour look and said, 'And we'll need it, *boshe moi*, we will!' He hitched up the white tape that hung in a big loop from his left shoulder. They would use it to mark the path they were hoping to clear.

Behind them the gun of the leading T-34 cracked suddenly. Vassily ducked instinctively. Next instant the shell exploded right on target, just in front of the wood. Almost immediately thick white smoke streamed upwards. For the next thirty minutes until his shells ran out, Tennov would continue one shell every two minutes, blinding the men holding the wood. By that time they *had* to be through.

'Come on,' the colonel commanded. 'You don't want to live for ever, do you, Vassily?'

'A couple of days more would be in order, colonel, all the same.' Obediently he advanced to where the first dead body lay crumpled, the legs and lower stomach horribly mutilated. Vassily gulped at the thought of *that* happening to him. Even if a man survived the wound, he wouldn't be a man any more. It was so frightening a vision that he shivered.

The colonel grinned softly. 'Louse run across your liver, Vassily?'

'Yes, colonel, a whole shitting squadron of them!' Then he, too, bent and started prodding the ground in front of him carefully with the bayonet, feeling the hot beads of sweat spring up unpleasantly all over his body. The misery had commenced.

Treading as if over eggshells, the two men advanced slowly into the minefield, prodding the ground to their left and right, unrolling the two white tapes to clear a path some three metres wide, the only sound that of their harsh, strained breathing and the steady crack of the cannon.

Twice they struck metal in the first five minutes, but quick examination showed the mines to be anti-personnel, and they were left in the ground. The German P2 S was too difficult to lift and besides the follow-up infantry would be riding on the deck of the tank. It was the antitank mines they were searching for. The colonel found the first one. Swiftly he worked his bayonet around the shape beneath the earth, while Vassily tensed at his side. 'Teller,' he announced after a moment. 'Let me handle it.'

He dropped the bayonet and cleared the deadly little prong with his bare hands. Then working outwards, he cleaned the soil from the top. 'Now for the tricky part,' he said grimly through gritted teeth.

Vassily knew what he meant. The Fritzes were cunning bastards. To prevent people like the colonel from removing the mine — and living — they often booby-trapped the damned things.

Now like some surgeon, carrying out a delicate operation within a patient's body, the outcome of which might mean life or death, the colonel ran his fingers underneath the mine, explaining his findings in tight little grunts like a surgeon might to the recording sister. 'No trip wire … no link wire either…'

Vassily sighed with relief. Often the Fritzes linked one mine to another or several others by a wire. If one were pulled without checking for links, the whole damn pattern exploded.

'No matchbox either,' the colonel said.

The matchbox was a little explosive device looking like a book matchbox. When the mine was lifted, the pressure on its spring was released and it exploded, exploding the mine too.

'All right, I'm going to lift and defuse.'

Vassily held his breath. If the colonel had made a mistake, they might well be both dead in one minute's time.

The colonel grunted and tugged. The mine came out easily. Nothing happened! An instant later he was screwing out the detonator and placing it and the mine outside the tape.

'All right?' he queried.

'Sure. Only the shit's dribbling down my right leg!'

The colonel laughed and moved on.

In the next ten minutes they lifted two further teller mines, one of them wired to another group hidden below the earth elsewhere. Slowly, painfully slowly, they got closer to the wood, now completely wreathed in thick white smoke. But not for long, the colonel told himself, his face now pale with strain and lathered in sweat. Soon Tennov's shells would run out and the Fritzes would begin to react.

Behind him now he could hear the rusty squeak of the tank's tracks as the T-34 laden with gulag rats and commanded by Major Tennov entered the minefield, carefully edging its way forward between the two white tapes. The colonel frowned. Soon the Fritzes would hear it too, and there would be some reaction, even though they would still be blinded by smoke.

'Try to move more quickly, Vassily,' he breathed, prodding the earth to left and right in a rapid arc with his bayonet, head cocked to one side, ears straining for that tell-tale scrape of metal on metal which would tell him he'd found another of the hellish devices. 'Tennov won't be able to keep up the smoke screen for ever. Time's running out!'□

'I'm doing my best, colonel,' Vassily answered almost angrily, not taking his eyes off the ground, jabbing his bayonet into the earth, sweating heavily, forcing himself to make each fresh step forward by a sheer effort of will, knowing that he could die violently at any moment.

They started to run into a belt of S-mines, anti-personnel devices filled with steel bearings, known aptly among the gulag rats as 'deballockers', for they exploded and threw their contents as high as the crotch with terrible effect.

They spent an agonizing five minutes worming their way through them, feeling the earth with their bare hands now like blind men groping for familiar ground knowing that the Fritzes could easily have planted a teller among them.

Then it happened. In the middle of the S-mines Vassily came across a teller with one of the anti-personnel devices tightly attached to it. For a moment he froze, unable to move, the sweat trickling coldly down the small of his back, knowing that if he moved the teller the deballocker could be activated by the slightest slip.

'What is it, man?' the colonel demanded urgently.

'Teller and S-mine linked, colonel,' he croaked.

'How?'

'Looks like S-mine on the right upper surface of the teller,' he heard himself saying in a voice he hardly recognized as his own.

'Shit!' the colonel cursed. He flung a glance at the green glowing dial of his wrist-watch. They had about five minutes left before Tennov ran out of smoke shells. Then they would be sitting ducks crouched out here in the middle of a minefield. 'You want me to have a —'

But Vassily had recovered his nerve already and had begun to tackle the problem himself.

The beads of sweat dripping from his eyebrows and almost blinding him, his fingers feeling as thick and as clumsy as some peasant blood-sausage, Vassily edged his way across the surface of the teller, following the slope until his fingers came to rest on the indented top of the S-mine.

Were they attached?... Were they attached? Was the question that burnt through his mind.

Nothing!

The surface was clear.

He took a deep breath, while the colonel watched, frozen into immobility, knowing that everything depended upon the other man now; *he* could do nothing.

Vassily edged his fingers underneath the teller like he had done under some plump pigeon's skirts in happier days, working them up over the knee, along the thigh until the stocking ended and then further, waiting for the girl's indignant explosion and hoping that perhaps this one time it would not come. Millimetre by millimetre they crept on, meeting no hindrance — no wire, no booby trap, no book match fuse. *Nothing!*

He breathed out hard and said in a little voice which he could hardly control. 'All right, colonel.'

'Then get the shit out — *quick!*'

Vassily did so, feeling drained of energy now; at the end of his tether.

Suddenly the shelling stopped. The colonel knew what had happened. Tennov had run out of smoke. He flashed a look to his front. The smoke was already beginning to drift away in the gloom. Any minute now they would be spotted. What was he going to do?

The cry of alarm made his mind up for him.

A machine-gun began to chatter angrily. A tracer cut the darkness, zipping flatly across the field. Behind them a soldier, perched on the tank, screamed and fell off. His body erupted in a terrible, violet burst of flame. He had fallen on a mine. His face shattered and he disintegrated. Bone and gore flew everywhere.

'Roll 'em!' the colonel roared at the frightened tank commander. 'For God's sake, move up now!'

'But the mines are not cleared —'

'Shit on them! *Move!*'

The cruel exhortation had its effect. The commander kicked the driver on the right shoulder, the signal for speed. He accelerated. Quickly the two officers swung themselves aboard, pushing aside the cowed, frightened gulag rats.

Snot-Face tried to hold them as long as he could; his men were too frightened of his evil, violent temper to break and run, in spite of the tank coming at them in the gloom, the men on its decks springing off and combing through the smouldering ruins.

'Come on, you sons of whores,' Snot-Face cried, 'do you want to live for ever? Counter-attack!'

Sobbing with fear, his men stumbled forward, throwing captured stick-grenades as they did so. A couple of the leading Russians disappeared in a burst of bright white light, severed limbs flailing in a whirling ball. But still the rest came on.

And then the tank came creaking round the corner. That did it. They came to a halt, as if they had run into an invisible wall. Snot-Face stopped too, screamed something that they could not make out over the roar of the tracks. Then he was running straight at the tank, grenade clutched in his hand. It was obvious what he was going to do. He was going to toss it into the turret or throw it at the driver's slot and blind him.

But Snot-Face never made it. The frightened gunner spotted him, just in time. He ripped off a frightened burst. Snot-Face skidded to a stop. For a moment he remained upright. But then his legs would support him no longer. He fell right in the path of the tank. The driver didn't hesitate. He ran over the fallen Pole, churning his body to pulp under the whirling tracks, curing Snot-Face's sinus trouble for ever. It was the signal his men had been waiting for. They broke, screaming and jostling each other in their attempt to get away from the metal monster. A minute later what was left of them had vanished into the surrounding forest.

The road to the west was open again.

CHAPTER 11

Standartenführer Kass fingered the long scar running down the side of his face from eye to mouth in a jagged zig-zag.

His chief-of-staff watched him, knowing that the general always touched the monstrous thing when he was tense or nervous; perhaps the scar meant something to him at such moments.

It did. As an eighteen-year-old student of engineering at the University of Vienna, whose father, a peasant from Upper Austria, had sent him to university at great sacrifice, he had desperately wanted *the* scar. This would be his entree into the world of the academics and ensure that the 'old gentleman' who had long left the university would provide him with the kind of job that would be his father's reward for his sacrifices. He had joined one of the duelling fraternities, not a very good one, but they duelled and if one could duel, in due course one received a scar. But on that May day when the doctor stopped the duel and he had been led away from the *paukboden* he had rushed to the nearest mirror to look at his face — and been shocked. The cut was little worse than a bad nick from a razor! Instinctively he knew it would heal up and leave hardly a mark. It was then that he made up his mind. Back in his shabby room, he had taken up his cut-throat razor with a hand that trembled badly and slashed the scar cut upwards and downwards, enlarging it till it dominated one side of his youthful, courageous face. He had never become an engineer, nor achieved academic respectability. The war and what had come after it had seen to that. But although he had fought everywhere, been wounded many times and gained enough 'tin', as he contemptuously called decorations for bravery, he knew that he had never again been as brave as he had been that afternoon with the razor. Since then whenever he was tense or nervous he instinctively touched the scar and thought of that day; now he had reason enough to feel nervous. He was not a sensitive man, but he could almost smell the tension that hung over the capital.

He glared through the window across the Vistula at Warsaw bathed in the afternoon heat. It was as if he could already see the dangers lurking there at every corner, though to any other observer the city seemed as if it had gone into a prolonged siesta.

'Anything wrong, sir?' the chief-of-staff asked finally, breaking the thick silence.

'Yes. Everything. They're up to something.'

'Who, sir?' the chief-of-staff asked, though he knew well enough what the general would reply.

'The Polacks, damn you, man!' the general snapped angrily and taking out a big handkerchief mopped his sweating brow. 'They know we're about beaten this side of the river if our people back at the Wolf's Lair don't pull a rabbit out of the hat pretty damn quick! They're preparing to rise. I know it.'

The chief-of-staff played him along, though he knew that the general was right. 'But how do you, sir?'

The *Standartenführer* marched across to his desk and snatched up the torn poster that lay there. He slapped it down on the window sill in front of the other man. 'Look at that! I found it stuck on the door of my quarters when I went out this morning. On the door of my quarters!'

The chief-of-staff stared at the poster. It depicted a death's head in a German helmet, super-imposed on a rifle bullet. Its message was pretty clear although he couldn't read the slogan in Polish.

The general could. 'And if you can't read the Polack, I'll tell you what it means. *Każady Pocisk — Jeden Niemiec*. A German for every bullet! And it's not only the poster. I can see them look at us when they think we're not watching them and there's hatred — naked hatred — in their eyes.'

The chief-of-staff sighed and stopped playing games. 'I suppose you're right, general.'

'I know I am,' he snorted and crumpled up the poster with a furious movement. 'All right, what news have you for me this afternoon, and I must warn you that damn green pea soup we had for lunch has set my stomach off growling, so make it good.'

The chief-of-staff shook his head sadly. 'I'm afraid, general, I would have to be the *lieber Gott* himself to bring you any good news these days.'

'Let's have it.'

'The Ivan column. It got through. The Poles attempted to stop it with a minefield, but the Ivans rushed them with tanks and the Poles made dust.'

Kass frowned and toyed with his scar again. 'All right, I know what you're going to say. *Viking* will have to stop them now.'

'I think it's the only way, sir. If we don't stop them and they reach the Vistula, they'll be reinforced just like that' — he clicked his fingers — 'especially if they can grab a bridgehead on the other bank. And remember, sir, they have got tanks.'

Kass absorbed the information with a nod. 'All the same, I'd like to keep the division intact up here. I hate the thought of having them spread all over the place, with roads and communications bad and the balloon going up over there in

Warsaw. Remember the old motto, *klotzen nicht klecksen*. Once the division is scattered, it'll be the devil's own job to get them together again, especially as half my cheeseheads, frogs, spaghetti-eaters and the rest don't speak German.'

The chief-of-staff laughed softly and sympathetically. 'Communications are a bit of a problem in the European Division'; he emphasized the words as if they were slightly dirty. 'What do you suggest then, sir?'

'This.' The general made up his mind. 'Just before Wolomin on the route they will obviously take, there is a ten per cent incline. It's a very tough gradient even for our Tigers.'

The chief-of-staff remembered the hill, wooded on both sides that snaked its way upwards seemingly interminably. 'Yes, I know it, sir.'

'Well, if we can pin them down there, we can get some sort of air reconnaissance to ascertain their exact position —'

'Yes, I think we could get a *Storch* out of the fly-boys, general.'

'Well, then we can send in the Goliaths.'

'The Goliaths!' the chief-of-staff exclaimed in delight. 'I'd never thought of them.'

'Of course, you hadn't,' the general replied, allowing himself a smile at his chief-of-staff's obvious surprise. 'That's why I command this division and you don't.' His grin vanished. 'All right, let's put some pepper in our britches, Hans. Get on to Air and then Major Reck of the Posen Military Academy; he's the chap who knows how to run the Goliaths. This time we're going to stop those Popovs for good...'

Standartenführer Kass was not the only one making final plans that afternoon. Squatting on a crate in the baking hot tobacco factory, a kilometre away from Kass's HQ, Bor listened attentively as Okulicki read out the full text of Stalin's radio message, ending with the heroic words, 'Poles, the time of liberation is at hand! Poles, to arms! There is not a moment to lose!'

The brigadier looked up from the paper.

'Who signed it?' Bor asked, carefully absorbing the rousing statement.

'Foreign commissar Molotov and that treacherous bastard Osobka Morawski!'

Bor said nothing for a moment. If the squat-faced Russian foreign minister, who had decided Poland's fate in 1939, and the head of the Moscow-sponsored Committee of National Liberation had signed the radio appeal, it meant very probably that it came from the Russian dictator himself. 'Well, Okulicki, what do you make of it?'

The brigadier laughed contemptuously. 'Easy. They're slowing down. The Russians are not going to make it to the Vistula, in spite of the fact that our people didn't stop them this morning. German resistance east of the river is hardening. So' — he drew a deep breath to add emphatically — 'the time has come for us to cross the Rubicon.'

There was a stifled gasp from the others.

'Explain carefully, please,' Bor said, already half-knowing what the other man was going to suggest but wishing to put off that terrible decision for as long as possible.

'I will,' said the brigadier, not quite able to conceal his contempt of what he thought to be Bor's slowness and indecision. 'The steam is going out of the Russian attack. Now they expect us to take some of the pressure off by rising in Warsaw.' He grinned. 'Let us do them that favour. After all we are *allies!*'

There were grins from the other officers present.

But Bor's long face remained its usual sad self. 'It's a damnably difficult decision to make, brigadier,' he said slowly. 'There must be at least half a million civilians in the city. There could be a tragedy.'

'They are Poles. They will expect to die for its freedom, Bor.'

Bor didn't seem to hear. 'The Germans are still not evacuating the city as we anticipated.'

'Let us speed them on their way — with a kick in the arse!' the brigadier cried coarsely.

For the first time in the meeting a new voice made itself heard. It was that of the handsome, if heavy-set Colonel Iranek-Osmecki, the Home Army's chief-of-intelligence. 'Bor,' he said, 'I have information from excellent sources that the Germans have massed four tank divisions, including the *Herman-Göring* and *SS Viking* on the other side of the river, perhaps to launch a counter-attack against the Red Army. In that case, it might well be a very long time before the Russians could enter Warsaw.'

Bor prepared to seize the idea and use it to his own purpose, but the brigadier was quicker. 'As usual, intelligence,' he sneered, 'is always seeing shadows and ghosts and nasty things in the middle of the night where there aren't any. If any general were to listen to intelligence, he'd never fight a damn battle!'

The colonel flushed. 'One has to be realistic, sir,' he said, controlling himself with difficulty. 'The Germans have been positively identified. My prognosis is that they are going to be used against the Russians.'

'All the better,' the brigadier snapped, knowing from the looks on the faces of the other officers that he had won. They had been waiting for action against the Germans for five years; they were prepared to wait no longer. 'Let the Fritzes and the Reds batter in each other's heads, while we take over our own capital. Besides if these German divisions of yours are prepared to attack, our rising would be just the thing the Reds need. We'd be able to cut their supply lines through Warsaw and any German defeat at the hands of the Reds would make that defeat a complete disaster.'

Bor took his point immediately. Of course it would. 'All right. It is done. *Stalo-sie*!'

The brigadier's broad, tough face lit up in a huge smile. 'When?' he demanded triumphantly.

'*Tomorrow, August the First*, 1944,' Bor answered simply.

Colonel Iranek-Osmecki crossed himself.

CHAPTER 12

They had been moving at a snail's pace all day now, partly to conserve Tennov's rapidly dwindling supply of fuel; partly because the colonel did not anticipate the Fritzes giving up so easily after the business at the village. He advanced warily, with scouts out on both sides, expecting another attack at any moment.

It was burningly hot. The grass, yellow, and parched, rippled with the heat haze and the sun was like a copper coin seen at the bottom of a hazy pool. The men spoke little, concentrating on the march, animated now and again when they stopped at some village for water or after a meal of cold beans and hard bread. Everyone was exhausted save the colonel. He was here, there and everywhere along the column, urging the beaten gulag rats on towards the west, with jokes, threats, even blows.

Vulf, who had decided he would accept the danger of being at point in Tennov's T-34 in exchange for not having to march with the rest, watched him in cynical, weary amazement. The man's energy seemed boundless and he could see why the colonel had become such a great leader of men before the war. He would simply not give up until he had got the last drop of effort out of his troops.

Tennov, his crimson face wet with sweat under his padded leather tanker's helmet, seemed to read Vulf's mind, for he said, wiping the back of his claw-like hand across his tight-skinned crippled face, 'Why in God's name did they ever put a man like that in the Gulag?' Vulf forced a parched smile.

'Comrade major, it is treason even to think a question like that.'

Tennov was neither afraid nor amused. 'But it's true,' he said with some heat. 'That man is ten times the patriot I am. What could have made them put him behind bars?'

'Not *them*,' Vulf corrected the puzzled major softly, 'but *him*.'

'Him?'

'Our Little Father in the Kremlin, comrade major — Marshal Stalin to be exact. No one knows his reasons for the things he does. A wrong choice of words, a misinterpreted look, a careless gesture — and, *puff!*' Vulf spread his soft white hands outwards, 'you're inside. It is the whim of the despot. No more, no less.' He smiled again at the puzzled look on Tennov's face. 'But don't let it worry you, comrade. It has always been thus in Russia and it is my belief it will always be that way. We are a people doomed, it seems, to suffer in silence. Fate.'

'But there is no such thing as a national fate!' Tennov protested. 'No nation is destined always to suffer the same blows over and over again. No, I disagree.'

'Of course,' Vulf admitted, warming a little to the discussion, 'no one can say that because the sun has risen every morning for the last so many million years, it will rise tomorrow again. But our history, comrade, seems to prove that we cannot escape the tyrant's yoke. The boyars, the tartars, the Cossacks, the czars, the communists. Relieved from one, we fall into the grasp of another monster. Perhaps we are just accident prone, secretly love the knout.' He grinned at a sweating Tennov and then his grin started to vanish slowly.

Tennov's expression changed too. 'What is it, Vulf?'

'A plane,' Vulf said hastily, 'coming in from the west.' He pointed up to the burning heavens.

A dark spot was coming towards them slowly, almost leisurely, as if the pilot had all the time in the world.

'Plane coming in!... Plane coming in!' the alarming cry ran down the column.

The colonel flung up his binoculars and focused them hastily. He recognized the high-wing monoplane with the big radial motor before he saw the black and white cross on its side. It was a Fiesler Storch. He dropped the glasses. 'Enemy recce plane,' he cried. 'Try to bring him down!' In spite of their exhaustion, the men reacted quickly enough. Professionally and expertly, man after man offered his back to his neighbour, who flung his rifle across the proffered shoulder and started firing from this rest; others fell on their back, raised their feet and jamming the tripods of their light machine-guns against their boots, used this as their mount. Lead cut the sky everywhere as the column stalled.

But the German pilot was either cunning or lucky. Flying at little more than 100 kilometres an hour and at almost ground level, he swung up one side of the column and then down the other, without apparently being struck once.

The colonel cursed and said, 'You'd think the damn Fritz was counting us.'

Vassily lowered his pistol and snapped in another magazine. 'He's probably doing just that, colonel,' he agreed and started firing at the plane once more.

But the pilot had already done his job. Waggling his wings a couple of times as if wishing them good-bye, he sped off the way he had come. In a few minutes he had disappeared altogether.

The colonel wiped the sweat off his forehead and stared angrily into nothing; then he said, 'All right, don't just stand like a lot of old peasants. You've seen a plane before. Mount up. Let's go on!'

Wearily the men complied. Once more the column set off across that burning, seemingly endless plain. But now their faces mirrored no longer just exhaustion, but also fear. What were the Fritzes up to?

Major Reck was a heavy-set, middle-aged man, who spoke carefully and somewhat pedantically as if it were important to make a few words go a long way; but then Major Reck had once been a teacher and he knew that the teaching day was a long one. In school one could afford to waste words. Now he lectured to the young soldiers from the *Viking* who had to come to assist him in the task of setting up the ambush at the ascent. He spoke in careful, slow words, as if he thought they were either not very intelligent or they might not understand if he explained too rapidly.

'It is our latest development,' he said, touching the object with his gleaming boot. 'In a way, a secret weapon you might call it, though of course not of the kind the Führer has promised us will win the war.' He beamed at them.

There was no answering light in the eyes of his listeners from the SS. They had been on the Eastern Front for nearly three years now; they knew there was no hope of winning. But they listened.

'Standing sixty centimetres with a length of some one and a half metres, it carries two hundred pounds' worth of explosive.' He opened the flap at the top of the miniature tank to show his listeners the high explosive packed inside.

'It is impervious to small arms' fire or hand grenades and as its speed is some thirty kilometres an hour, it is pretty hard for an enemy cannon to range in on it. In short, soldiers, it is somewhat of a wonder weapon.' Again he beamed at his listeners.

'How is it controlled?' one of his listeners asked in the thick guttural German of a Dutchman.

'Sometimes by radio, but mostly by cable.'

'And its range?' the Dutchman asked again.

It was the kind of question that delighted Major Reek's schoolmaster's heart. It gave him that opportunity, one that is always seized by teachers, to show off his knowledge. 'Some eight hundred metres by radio — and in the case of this one, controlled by cable, exactly seven hundred and fifty.'

Now the soldiers were impressed, and Major Reck knew why. They could control the mini-tank from behind cover, steering it to its victim with little or no danger to themselves. It was the kind of battle-winning weapon that frontline soldiers dreamed of. 'So you see, soldiers, employed in large enough numbers — and we have some twenty at our disposal,' he indicated the weapons lined up neatly behind them in the cover of the pines — 'our little friends can sweep away any kind of obstruction. *Also unser Goliath,*' he concluded benignly.

The soldiers began to chatter excitedly about the 'wonder weapon', and he let them, while he assessed the ground, making his dispositions, telling himself the place was perfect for an ambush, allowing himself the momentary luxury of imagining what the successful outcome of this operation would mean for him: the Knight's Cross or the Iron Cross or at least the Cross-in-Gold. That would mean promotion, and military rank always stood one in good stead in teaching. He'd make *Schuldirektor* yet.

He was roused from his reverie by the faint drone of an aircraft. All eyes flashed to the east, trying to make out the plane's shape against the burning sky.

'*Storch!*' the Dutchman cried, 'one of ours!'

Reck breathed out a little sigh of relief. Up to June he had been in the west and he had come to know and fear the tommy and amis *jabos*.

A moment later the Storch came zooming in just over their heads so that they ducked instinctively. A tiny parachute popped open and came floating down slowly, while the plane sped on its way back to Warsaw, to land almost at the middle-aged major's feet.

Reck opened it at once, read the hastily scribbled note, took a quick glance at the cross marked on the map to indicate their position, then shouted with unaccustomed haste and energy for him. 'They're an hour's march away — the Ivans. Come on, let's get these little fellows set up.' He beamed at them, in spite of a suddenly nervous pumping of his heart. '*This time Goliath will undoubtedly knock the shit out of David...*'

CHAPTER 13

The T-34s, their engines roaring in low gear, struggled up the steep incline, exhausts pouring out smoke, tank commanders furiously waving their flags at each other, warning one another to keep their distance.

The colonel was up front with Major Tennov, who kept swinging the turret from side to side suspiciously, his nerves on edge, knowing that his beloved tanks strung out on the steep ascent, grinding upwards at ten kilometres an hour were sitting ducks for any anti-tank gunners who might be hidden in the thick pine woods on both sides of the pass.

More than once the colonel patted him soothingly on his skinny shoulder and said, 'It's too obvious, major. They wouldn't attack us here. Besides they'd need armour to take you and your precious T-34s. And armour can't operate in those woods.'

But Tennov was not to be appeased. His nerves on edge, he scanned the woods, as if he half expected Fritzes to come pouring out of them at any moment, saying, 'Be prepared for anything. Once I wasn't. That's how I got a kisser like this.' He pointed to his lobster-red face.

The colonel gave up and concentrated on his own problems. According to Tennov he had fuel left for another five kilometres at the most. That meant they would have to abandon the tanks once they had rushed the little town on the other side of the hill. He had thought of suggesting to Tennov that his tankers should share out their fuel so that the gulag rats had the cover of half-a-dozen T-34s till they reached the Vistula, but he had dismissed the idea almost immediately, knowing that Tennov would not abandon his crews. As soon as their fuel ran out, Tennov would stop and dig in in a hull-down position to wait for the follow-up to reach them. And in a way it would be better, the colonel reasoned, for the gulag rats to go on alone. Without the tanks they would be able to sneak up to the river through the thickening German positions he expected to find on the east bank. Tanks were becoming a hindrance; they could be easily spotted from the air. Little groups of infiltrators on foot were more difficult to pin-point.

But assuming they reached the river, what then? The marshal hadn't said anything about that problem. How would they be able to hold their positions against the customary German counter-attack without heavy weapons and armour? The colonel shrugged and, like the good soldier he was, dismissed the problem. That would be taken care of when it arose.

He looked at his rats. They were slumped down everywhere on the tanks' burning decks, snoring or blinking lazily into the red ball of the sun. They looked at the end of their tether, he told himself. But then it had been a long haul, with little water and less food. Once he reached the Vistula, he reasoned that the marshal would throw in everything he had to reach him and gain the honour of forcing the first bridgehead across the Vistula. There, there would be food and drink enough — for those who survived.

Tennov nudged him hard. 'What is it, major?' he asked, jolted out of his reverie.

'Can you hear that noise?'

'Noise? I can't hear anything except the racket these sardine cans of yours are kicking up?'

Tennov, looking suddenly even more worried, cocked his head to one side and lifting his helmet flap, strained. 'No, colonel, it's something else. Another noise.'

'I can't hear anything,' he began.

But Tennov, the younger man with the more acute hearing, cut him short. 'Over there to the right. It's coming from somewhere there!' □

Then the colonel heard it too, a strange metallic whirring sound, reminding him strongly of the electric trams of his youth in Moscow. For a moment he did not react. Then he swung his eyes from left to right, searching every millimetre of ground in front of the forest in the manner of the battle-experienced soldier that he was.

'There!' Tennov cried, stretching out his arm, in the same instance that the colonel spotted it himself: a squat steel shape, about the height of a small child, crashing its way out of the foliage and beginning to crawl towards the tanks in a frighteningly purposeful manner.

'*Boshe moi*,' he cursed, 'what in God's name is it?' Tennov shook his head helplessly. 'Never seen anything like that before.' He hesitated. 'But it looks … looks like a small tank.'

'But where is its cannon?' the colonel objected. 'Where's the crew?' He swallowed hard, a cold finger of fear tracing its way down his spine at the eerie apparition. 'Besides what could a damn little thing like that do against a normal T-34? Why … why…' he stuttered, 'it's no bigger than a kid's toy!'

'You're right,' Tennov gulped. 'But it's German. Of that I'm sure. We haven't got anything like that in the Red Army. And if it's Fritz, it spells trouble for us.' Tennov hesitated no longer. He raised his signal flags and began wiggling them rapidly, and by doing so he made a fatal mistake; for his order to his T-34s strung out along that steep gradient was 'STOP!'

'What are you doing?' the colonel queried, not taking his eyes off the monster which was now crawling across rocks and the rough earth, trailing what looked like cable behind it, directly towards a T-34 half-way down the column.

'I've ordered the T-34s to take up a defensive position,' Tennov replied and shouted something to his gunner through his mike. 'We'll sit it out here.'

'But...' the colonel began and then gave up as Tennov's gunner cranked the turret round, directing his cannon at the monster. Behind him the others did the same.

Now another of the strange little crawling things emerged from the forest to their right and almost immediately another — and another!

The colonel cupped his hands around his mouth and yelled. 'Dismount — dismount, gulag rats, and get into that ditch over there!' He knew he had to protect the tanks against this strange new weapon, for instinctively he realized it was a weapon.

Hurriedly the rats dropped from the tank decks and took up their positions, weapons at the alert.

Now the crawling metal objects were some 500 metres away and the colonel could see the cables they trailed behind them quite clearly. He guessed that they were being controlled by them, something like the remote-controlled toys he remembered from before the war. Next to him, Tennov had ordered his gunner to take aim at the closest. The response had been a good dealing of cursing from the gunner, but now he had his big 75mm cannon depressed as far as it would go, still protesting that the 'shit things' were too small for him to get at. Tennov rapped angrily, 'Fire!'

Hastily both he and the colonel threw up their glasses. For a few seconds they could follow the white burr of the armour-piercing shell as it zapped through the air, then it was lost. A moment later there was the impact of solid shot hitting the earth beyond the tank; the sudden flurry of flying soil and pebbles told them that the gunner had overshot the crawling object by at least fifty metres.

Tennov struck the side of the turret with rage. The monster was crawling ever closer, completely unscathed. 'What in heaven's name can we do against them?' he cried.

Below in the ditch, Captain Weis ordered a light mortarman to 'put an egg on it!'

Hastily the mortarman knelt and clasped the curved base plate of the little mortar to his right knee. His mate slipped in the small bomb. The mortarman spun the firing wheel and closed his eyes instinctively as they all did, while his mate turned his face, thrusting his fingers in his ears against the blast. The muzzle flashed violet flame. A thump. And the ugly little bomb was wobbling through the burning sky up and upwards, before falling with ever increasing speed directly upon the second monster. There was a bright flash of flame. Shrapnel howled everywhere, the gulag rats cried, '*direct hit! You've shat right on him!*' as smoke wreathed the thing.

But their triumph was short-lived. When the smoke cleared, they could see that the monster, its steel deck a gleaming silver now with the gouges torn out of the metal by the shrapnel, had not deviated from its course, crawling ever nearer to the stalled tanks with grim, inhuman, frightening deliberation.

Tennov gulped. '*Boshe moi*, colonel!' he gulped. 'The buggers are … frightening! Worse than the Fritz Tigers. At least you can hit them!'

The colonel did not answer. His mind was racing. Due to the unfortunate position of the tanks, they would not be able to bring their guns to bear until it was too late; the Fritzes had picked their ambush site well. But if the tanks could not stop the strange monsters, could his infantry? He doubted it. The things seemed impervious to mortar fire and that was the heaviest weapon the gulag rats possessed. He thought of the wires controlling them in the same instant that Weis rose to his feet and cried, 'Section One — *after me*!' He raced forward, followed by a rough skirmish line of rats, heading straight for the crawling monsters, his intention obvious: he was going to try to cut the control wires!

Almost immediately the Fritzes covering the Goliaths in the woods realized what the rats were up to. Small arms' fire broke out. Slugs howled off the rocks and outcrop, as the rats doubled in and between the strange rumbling monsters, heading for the cables, but taking more and more casualties all the time.

But the dark-faced Volga German seemed to bear a charmed life. Like an American footballer, the colonel once remembered seeing in a pre-war newsreel, he zig-zagged violently, legs and arms pumping away, slugs kicking up little violent spurts of earth at his heels.

The colonel felt his hands gripped to tight sweating fists as Weis got ever nearer to the closest monster, while behind him man after man dropped to the ground, dead and wounded.

Would he be able to stop it?

Leathern-lunged, his heart pounding crazily, Weis came level with the monster and heard the slithering of the cable it dragged behind it. Ignoring the howl of the bullets off its metal sides, he wondered frantically how he was going to do it.

Hidden by the pines some 500 metres away, the middle-aged German major saw the danger immediately. If the lone man managed to sever the cables, there might be other Popov glory-hunters who would attempt the same trick. 'Get him boys,' he roared to the riflemen covering their comrades operating the cables. 'Get the Ivan bastard!'

As one they swung round and started to direct their concentrated fire on the lone figure running parallel with the Goliath now.

Weis did not seem to notice the fire.

'Do it … do it, man! Now,' the colonel willed the running man. He knew that Weis would not survive that concentrated fire much longer. 'Jump it!'

Next to him Tennov was muttering the first prayer he had uttered since he had put religion behind him to join the Young Pioneers.

Weis took one last deep breath and dived forward, two hands outstretched. They gripped the cables, feeling the rough wire cut deep into his palms and the instant drag-and-tug at his shoulder muscles as the monster started to drag his prone body across the rough earth. He hung on grimly, exerting all his strength to tug out the cables, cursing obscenely, wincing at the pain as his body was towed over rocks and sharp obstructions, like a rider being dragged in the stirrup by a horse that had thrown him.

Suddenly he dropped back, the cables clutched in his bleeding, ripped palms as they came away. He lay there gasping in the dust, while the monster rolled powerlessly to a stop. It was just then that the burst of well-aimed machine-gun fire ripped open his back and Weis died.

But the captain's sacrifice was in vain. In the same instant that he died, the first Goliath slammed into a stationary T-34 half-way down the road. There was a loud echoing silence which seemed to go on forever. The Goliath exploded. Two hundred pounds of packed explosive burst into full, furious force at the T-34's side. It split like an over-ripe tomato under the blow of a heavy hammer. Men and metal flew high into the air in the whirling frantic ball of fire and smoke.

'The road's blocked!' Tennov gasped, as the fireball cleared and he saw that what remained of the two vehicles, a shattered mess of metal, prevented the other T-34s from moving on.

The colonel grasped the situation at once, as the next Goliath exploded taking the T-34 stalled at the rear of the column with it. The Fritzes were going to attempt to prevent them moving forwards or backwards so that they could pick off the stationary tanks at leisure. If they didn't move within seconds, they were finished. 'Tennov, you've got to move. At the double! We'll be trapped otherwise!'

'I know ... I know,' Tennov gasped. 'But my people?'

'They'll have to make out the best they can,' the colonel rasped and blew three shrill blasts on his whistle, the signal for his rats to start abandoning their positions. 'Let's get what is left moving and over the hill! In a minute they're going to direct one of those shitty monsters at this tank. Look!'

Already one of the Goliaths had been directed to change course by its controllers hidden in the forest and was beginning to crawl uphill, parallel with the road, obviously heading for the command tank.

Tennov made a quick decision. It would be his last, but he had always told himself that he would never survive this war. Besides which girl would want him with his face? Girls he had enough at present. But now he was a hero. After the war he would be only a 'war-wounded', one of those faceless, legless, armless ones — the basket-cases as they were sometimes called — who would be hidden away in some remote hospital until some time when either death or the plastic surgeons released them. 'No, colonel. I can't run and leave my people. Besides we've only got fuel for a few more kilometres.'

'Perhaps we can loot some juice down in the town and then—'

'Doubt it,' Tennov cut him off curtly. 'My mind is made up. Get your men moving — at the double. I'll tackle them.'

'What?'

'You heard.' Tennov seemed almost happy. 'Ram them like a destroyer does a sub.'

'But that would be sheer suicide!' the colonel snorted.

Tennov shrugged easily and grinned with that monstrous lobster-red face of his. 'A short life and a sweet one, don't they say, though I don't think I'll make a particularly pretty corpse with this kisser of mine... Now be off with you ... *gulag rat!*'

He pushed, and caught off his guard, the colonel fell over the side into the dust where his gulag rats were already massing.

A moment later the T-34's motors roared into violent life.

'Stop!' the colonel yelled in vain.

Tennov, busy with his signal flags ordering the remaining T-34s to follow him, grinned down and although he could not hear the words, the colonel could read them. They were 'Good-luck, gulag rats.'

The T-34 swung round to face the enemy. For a moment it teetered at the edge of the raised road, its 400HP engines roaring, blue smoke streaming from its exhausts; then with a burst of speed it descended, showering the staring rats with dirt and pebbles and began to race for the nearest Goliath, followed by the survivors. In a V-formation like keen-prowed destroyers, their wake a stream of dust on both sides, they headed for the last encounter.

The colonel waited no longer. Tennov's sacrifice must not be in vain. 'At *the double... Follow me, gulag rats!*' he cried above the scream of engines going full out and the crack of 75mm cannon.

Five minutes later they were over the brow of the hill, breath coming like that of ancient asthmatics, falling exhausted into the dust, the only sound the long dying echo of T-34 after T-34 as Tennov's tankers fought their last battle.

The gulag rats had survived once again.

CHAPTER 14

August the first, 1944, dawned bright, clear, sunny and cool, though the red ball of the sun edging up over Warsaw's skyline promised that it would be a very hot day in the Polish capital.

It was the kind of a day that made people feel good, that there was still hope for the wicked old world, that there was a future. People nodded to each other as they walked to work in the streets of the capital and said 'good morning' to total strangers.

Even the German patrols, which were everywhere, did not seem quite so oppressive and threatening as they did normally; and now and again when they thought their superiors weren't watching the young soldiers winked or even whistled at the pretty girls in their flowered dresses and wooden shoes hurrying off — apparently — to their office jobs. Sometimes the girls smiled back and forgot — momentarily — that hidden in their bags and briefcases were pistols and parts of Sten guns with which they would soon shoot down these same smiling open-faced innocent young men.

In his shabby civilian clothes Bor shuffled down the untidy streets heading for his HQ in Pavia Street which ended in a cul-de-sac. He, too, enjoyed the sun and told himself that Nature herself seemed to bless the Polish cause. It was a suitable day to grasp back Poland's freedom. He passed the back of the burnt-out ghetto, in which the Jews had fought and died the previous year, walked by the German pillbox guarding the access road, held, he noted by a very wide-awake German machine-gun team, grasped instinctively the little pistol hidden deep in the pocket of his raincoat, and then stopped in front of the butter-coloured Kemmler tobacco factory. He gave the usual knock and was received excitedly by his waiting staff.

Everywhere there was controlled chaos. Technicians were setting up radios so that as soon as the revolt started they would be able to communicate with the world. NCOs were handing out the home-made *filipinka* grenades to the defence platoon. 'Pigeons', as they called the female snipers, none of them older than twenty, were busy oiling and checking their rifles, adjusting their telescopic sights. Staff officers scribbled away furiously, preparing the many messages which would be raced across the airways once the uprising had commenced.

Bor nodded his approval and then accepted the message his staff had prepared for him. It would be flashed all over the capital, Poland, the world, once the battle began. His eyes danced from word to word, from line to line, with growing approval. 'Soldiers of the capital!... I have today issued the order which you desire ... for open warfare against Poland's age-old enemy, the German invader... After nearly five years of ceaseless and determined struggle ... carried out in secret ... you stand openly with arms in hand ... to restore freedom in our country ... and to mete out fitting punishment to the German criminals ... for the terror and crime committed by them on Polish soil...'

He handed back the message to the waiting officer, who was surprised to see that tears glistened in the old man's eyes. 'It is a fitting message,' Bor said thickly. 'You have done well. Now...'

Colonel Geibel, commander of Warsaw's SS and Police units, listened attentively to the excited officer's voice on the telephone as befitted a good policeman. But the connection was bad and he was worried that the Polacks might have put a tap on his phone, so he had to keep interrupting the *Luftwaffe* with 'what did you say … please repeat that, would you?'

And then finally he had it. The man was sleeping with a Polish woman, which was basically illegal for a German officer; therefore it took some courage on the man's part at the other end of the line to call Geibel like this and pass on information which could incriminate him. The woman had warned him, pleaded with him to leave the capital by five o'clock this afternoon.

'Are you sure she said five?' Geibel said.

'Quite certain, Colonel,' the *Luftwaffe* man answered.

'And why?'

'Because the whole of Warsaw is going to rise against the Germans at that time.'

'The whole of Warsaw?'

'Her exact words, sir.'

For a long moment Geibel was silent while he pondered the news. It fitted in with his own theories. That morning out in the suburb of Zoliborz a carload of his policemen had bumped into a group of Polacks openly carrying arms. There had been a running fight and suddenly the whole suburb had exploded into violence. In the end he had been forced to ask for troops and it had taken them three hours to subdue the trouble with heavy losses on both sides.

'What am I to do, sir?' the *Luftwaffe* officer broke into his thoughts.

Geibel chuckled, an unusual sound for that torturer. 'I would suggest, my dear fellow, that you pull it out very quickly, don't even bother to wipe it, and *run like hell…*'

General Reiner Stahel, the new commander of all troops in Warsaw, listened attentively to what Geibel had to say. He was new to Warsaw, indeed he had only been in the Polish capital twenty-four hours, and from his position in the Bruehl Palace everything seemed very calm. Yet he knew, too, that Geibel was an old hand in Poland and what his spies couldn't find out, his torturers could. The SS colonel was a person to be taken seriously. So he did not interrupt the man on the other end of the phone.

Easing his collar against the sultry heat and listening as the policeman poured on the misery, he realized that the balloon really was to go up. Something had to be done. The Führer personally had entrusted Warsaw's defences to him in this hour of crisis; and he didn't want to let Hitler down. His career depended upon it after all.

'All right,' he said finally, 'I'll put my defence force on alarm stage one. We'll cut the city into five control zones and I'll see what I can do about bringing heavy flak to be used in a ground role…'

Colonel Geibel let him run on, barely listening. Typical soldier, he told himself, thinking in terms of a nice tidy little battle between himself and another officer just like him, educated in similar doctrines in similar military schools, reading the same textbooks, employing the same tactics and the same theories. Just like that. Then suddenly he had had enough. 'With all due respect, *Herr general*,' he interrupted Stahel's flow of words and there was no respect whatsoever in his harsh policeman's voice, 'what is going to happen here today is not going to be a battle. It's going to be sheer slaughter!' And before the general could stutter his protest, he slammed the phone back on the receiver.

Now it was almost time.

Bor looked at his wristwatch for the umpteenth time. Would it never be five o'clock? Still forty-five minutes to go.

Then it happened. Germans in full field-marching order started to stream into the house opposite. Bor knew instinctively that the Fritzes had realized what was afoot. He ordered his defence platoon to take up their positions. Still he could not quite bring himself to order his men to open fire. The Germans did the job for him.

A slug howled through the window at the far end of the factory. Why it was fired no one ever found out. Were the Fritzes just jumpy? Did they know what the Kemmler factory housed? Were they firing on anything that was Polish? Whatever the cause, they had their answer soon enough. One of the pigeons hurled her *filipinka* into a group of German infantry assembled in the street below.

It exploded with a thick crump. German grenadiers went flying high into the air, arms and legs flailing with the force of the explosion, and at once there was firing everywhere. It spread from street to street, from quarter to quarter, ever outwards until the whole of Warsaw was ablaze. *The uprising had begun!*

'*Was … was haben Sie gesagt?*' Heinrich Himmler, head of the SS, bellowed into the telephone, chinless face paler than ever. Stahel repeated what he had just said, realizing that the feared Himmler, the man who commanded the whole National Socialist terror machine throughout German-occupied Europe, was afraid, clearly afraid.

Himmler clapped his hand to his forehead in that dramatic German gesture of surprise and grabbed at his pince-nez the next moment to prevent it from being dislodged from his sharp schoolmaster's nose. 'It can't be true!' he exclaimed.

'But it is true, *Reichsführer*,' Stahel persisted and holding the telephone away from his ear, allowed the man far away in the Führer's HQ to hear the snap and crackle of small arms fire outside. 'Since seventeen hundred hours this afternoon, the Poles have been attacking us.'

Himmler was convinced. 'Heaven, arse and cloudburst,' he cursed, although he was normally a prim and proper individual, not given to cursing. 'What audacity! But by God's name, that Polack pack will pay for this!' He slammed down the phone, his sallow face flushed with rage.

Three hours later the black-clad figure of the *Reichsführer SS* hurried from his big black Horch directly to the wooden hut in the East Prussian Führer HQ, used as Hitler's private quarters.

It was late, but then the Führer rarely went to sleep before two in the morning. Besides he was having one of his usual gas attacks and even the sixty pills a day prescribed for him didn't seem to be helping him this evening. Thus Himmler found him walking up and down the panelled bare room, holding his noisily grumbling stomach, pausing only to fart yet once again.

Himmler, a fastidious man, wrinkled his nose at the smell, but over the years he had become accustomed to it. Hitler had stunk of rotten eggs ever since he had known him.

Almost apathetically Hitler listened to Himmler's account of what was happening in Warsaw, farting every now and again, but saying nothing.

It was an opportunity that Himmler took gladly. He liked giving speeches and with Hitler he rarely got the chance to do so. Now he spoke at length, his sallow face flushed with genuine rage, his pig's eyes behind the gold-rimmed pince-nez blazing. 'I know the moment is not opportune for a detailed historical perspective. But what the Poles are doing is a blessing in disguise. Within a few days the whole problem in Warsaw will be sorted out — to our advantage. The Polish intelligentsia will be wiped out. That dastardly people which has blocked our way eastwards for a century, which has been a thorn in our side since the First Battle of Tannenberg five hundred years ago will no longer be a problem for us or our descendants.'

Hitler farted and groaned slightly. Still he said nothing. Himmler rambled on, his fury reaching its crescendo. '*Mein Führer* I request your permission to destroy Warsaw totally. I want to destroy each house block so that the Polacks can't dig in. I want to destroy their museums, their palaces, their libraries, their art galleries,' Himmler gasped for breath. 'I want to raze Warsaw to the ground, to turn it into ash and rubble, *to destroy it!*'

He paused, his skinny body shaking with the effort of so much excited talk and waited expectantly. The Führer did not speak. His eyes were glazed and apathetic still. He could well have been dead save for the trembling of his right hand and the constant breaking of wind. Himmler waited impatiently. Outside there was no sound except for the crunch of the sentry's boots on the gravel and the soft pat-pat of the guard-dog which accompanied him. Finally Himmler could contain himself no longer. '*Mein Führer*, what is your decision?' he blurted out.

Hitler seemed to see him for the first time. His voice husky and without emotion, he said: 'Wipe them out...'

CHAPTER 15

Marshal of the Soviet Union Konstantin Rokossovsky sweated. The sun of the burningly hot August day had long gone down and the heat had vanished; still he sweated as if it were thirty degrees. He dabbed his cologne-soaked handkerchief against his lofty brow and asked himself why this always happened when he was waiting for a telephone call from Old Leather-Face. Was it hate? Or was it fear? Miserably he concluded it was fear.

He was scared of what the dictator in the Kremlin could do to him, a man who commanded an army of half a million men. He could order thousands of men to their death each day, could conquer huge chunks of territory for Russia, was lord and master of every man, woman, child over an area as big as the Ukraine; yet he trembled when he was called to receive a telephone call from Stalin. Rokossovsky dabbed his brow once again and waited, his mind racing, wondering what was coming.

Was he going to be told that his hated rival Marshal Konev was to be given the honour of making the running for the Vistula, now that the gulag rats had done the dirty work and his army had nearly reached them? Was it something to do with the unconfirmed report that had reached him an hour before that the Poles had revolted in Warsaw? Or was it something more sinister? Was Stalin going to take his army away from him and send him back to the camps?

He groaned aloud, not caring that most of his senior staff officers were in the room and were watching him. He dabbed his sweating brow once again.

Then the phone rang. He jumped as if shot. With a hand that trembled slightly, he picked it up and trying to control his voice, said: 'Rokossovsky.'

'Ah, my dear Rokossovsky,' that unmistakable Georgian voice said. 'Good evening, comrade.'

'Good evening, comrade,' the marshal found himself saying, knowing by the little pleasantry that his head was not for the block this particular evening.

'I thought I'd call you and see how things were going on your front,' Stalin opened in that usual oblique manner of his.

'Excellently, comrade,' Rokossovsky said promptly, glad to be able to get on to military matters, though he knew quite well that Stalin was superbly informed on what went on at the front by the Stavka. Skilfully and expertly he filled in the details of his army's advance that day, going down as far as corps level and once, in the case of a particularly effective attack to that of a division, while Stalin listened in silence, not in the least interested in such trivia, as Rokossovsky knew.

Finally he finished and waited for what must surely come, mopping his dripping brow.

To his surprise, Stalin still did not come to the point. Instead he asked, 'And where is your point, comrade marshal?'

Surprised Rokossovsky answered. 'Between Treblinka and the Vistula, though I have a small group on the east bank of the river itself.'

Stalin absorbed the information and the sweating army commander could visualize him in the big room at the Kremlin, his dark eyes narrowed and cunning, but revealing nothing, sucking at that damned curved pipe of his.

'You know that your point will be attacked by the Germans tomorrow?' he asked suddenly.

If the dictator expected him to be surprised now, Rokossovsky was not going to give him that pleasure. 'Yes,' he snapped back, 'elements of the *SS Viking* Panzer Division and the *Hermann-Göring* Panzer Division are massing out there. My staff and I expect an attack to come in just after dawn. It is standard operating procedure with their elite divisions. Probably without an artillery barrage too.'

'You are prepared for a surprise attack then, comrade marshal?'

'Yes, comrade. They won't catch us off our guard. I have two whole corps and a corps of armour on that flank.' His voice filled with pride. 'They won't get through my army.'

'But your army will be undoubtedly forced to stop and re-group after this attack,' there was something so sly about Stalin's voice that the soldier did not know whether this words were meant as a question or a statement of fact. After a moment's hesitation he decided they were a question.

'No, comrade,' he answered. 'We shall be able to handle it without any need to halt in place.'

'But you will.' There was iron in Stalin's voice now.

'What did you say, comrade?' Rokossovsky gasped.

'I think you heard me, comrade.' There was no denying the threat. 'Publicly it will be given out that the Second White Front has run into very serious enemy opposition between Treblinka and the Vistula. As a consequence its drive for the river must cease for the present while new troops are brought up.'

'But why?' Rokossovsky asked, so surprised that he was no longer afraid of the monster in the Kremlin.

'There is no need for me to tell you, though I doubt if your thick soldier's head will comprehend my politics.'

Rokossovsky flushed angrily and the knuckles of his hand holding the telephone turned white, but he said nothing.

'Those Polish fascists in Warsaw have revolted against the Germans as we have been expecting them to do all week. Now they've gone off at half-cock and the Germans are going for them. They've pissed in the soup, now they must drink it. So, we stand at the sidelines like spectators at a game of football and watch the Polacks and the Fritzes knock each other's turnips to pieces. When that job has been completed, your army can advance and take the capital. It will be as easy as lifting your little finger. Now do you understand?'

Rokossovsky heard himself saying that he did.

'*Horoscho*,' Stalin snapped. 'Now see to it that not one single Russian soldier crosses that river until I give the word. We are playing for high stakes, Rokossovsky, and I am not going to allow some stupid tin soldier to lose the game for me. Remember well what I have said, or you will answer to me for it...'

Suddenly the line went dead, leaving a trembling Rokossovsky staring at the phone, as if it contained something of importance, like a character at the end of the first act of a second-rate play.

The colonel was exhausted, but he slept badly, tossing and turning in the slit trench he had dug on the river bank, his mind racing with the terrible pictures of the last week: the senior sergeants shooting the men against the wall; the stench of that camp and the old man quavering, 'The best thing was to carry the bodies, then you could take their bread ration. The dead don't need to eat, do they?' Tennov's terribly burnt face cracking into a pathetic mockery of a smile as he turned to face the Goliaths. Death and destruction, horror and terror everywhere.

'Comrade colonel,' the voice seemed to come from far away. A hand touched him lightly and he was awake at once, pistol already out from underneath his head.

It was Vulf.

He sat up licking parched lips. 'What is it, Vulf? Bad news?'

'I suppose so.'

'Well, come on then, man, piss or get off the pot!'

Vulf gave him his twisted smile. 'You turn a neat phrase, comrade colonel.'

The colonel ignored the remark and waited.

'Radio message just came through from army HQ. The marshal personally.' □

Hastily the colonel rose to his feet, really alert now. 'Yes, go on. What did it say?'

'From one gulag rat to another, hold your ears stiff, because there is to be no relief.'

'No relief?' the colonel exploded.

'There is more to come, colonel … the army has broken off its advance to relieve us because it is expecting a strong German counter-attack. We are to hold out here on the river the best we can. The marshal seemed to indicate that you ought, if you could, hang on to the position here until the army is in a position to advance once more.' Vulf stalled for a moment and then he let the Old Man have the sting-in-the-tail. 'Finally in no circumstances *whatsoever* — and he emphasized that word as if his life depended upon it — is Punishment Battalion 333 to have any contact with the Poles over there in Warsaw or make any attempt to cross the Vistula.'

With a groan, feeling his stiffness now the colonel rubbed his back and put on his helmet. 'But what does it mean, Vulf? Why stop now after all the effort, the blood, the deaths?'

'Politics?' Vulf answered simply.

'What do you mean?' The colonel snapped at him angrily, 'Politics?'

By way of a reply, Vulf curled his finger at the colonel and said, 'Come, colonel.'

Puzzled, the colonel followed him and they scrambled up the bank, through the trees which fringed it, to the height overlooking the river.

The Vistula danced crazily in the ruddy, reflected light that came from the city on the other side. Over the city itself searchlights cut the gloom with icy blades, signal rockets exploded in flashes of red and green and there was no mistaking the ugly snap and crackle of small arms fire, punctuated every now and again by the solid thump of cannon.

Vulf spoke finally, softly and quite undramatically. 'Politics means that that over there must end first before we can advance again. Warsaw must die.' Then he gave a little laugh. 'And I suppose, thinking about it now, we gulag rats will be dead too by then.'

'Dead,' the colonel echoed tonelessly, his face hollowed out to a blood-red skull by the light from across the river, 'dead…'

BOOK TWO: *THE DECISION*

CHAPTER 1

With a roar of its enormous engines, the Tiger burst through the trees, snapping off' pines as easily as if they were matchsticks. Behind it was the usual 'grape', a tight bunch of SS infantry clad in their camouflaged overalls, crouched low, splattered with mud and pebbles as the driver revved and the tracks started to revolve more quickly.

The colonel, from his position on the bank, threw up his binoculars. To his front he could hear Captain Vassily crying faintly, 'Stand to ... stand to everywhere... The Fritzes are coming again!'

The colonel swung his glasses, from left to right. Dark shapes popped up into the gleaming circles of calibrated glass. Vassily's men were rousing themselves from their exhausted sleep at the bottom of their foxholes. This would be the sixth attack in the last forty-eight hours and the men were about at the end of their tether; and this time the Fritzes were coming in with a tank. And what a tank! A seventy-two ton monster as big as a cottage, armed with a tremendous 88mm cannon. The colonel bit his lip. What could Vassily do against a monster like that. He stared with horrified fascination as the Tiger ground ever closer to Vassily's slit-trench line, its long overhanging cannon swinging from side to side like some primeval predator searching out its prey. How long would it be before Vassily's rats sprang from their holes, threw away their weapons and started pelting back to the mainline on the river bank?

Vassily, in the centre of the line, had the same thought too. His handsome face taut and pale, he watched anxiously as the Tiger came nearer and nearer; then he flung a glance at his gulag rats. He didn't need to be a mind-reader to know that they were frightened, terribly frightened. Their eyes gleamed with a wet sheen, as if they might break down and sob at any moment, and their pale, cracked lips trembled continually. Vassily said a silent prayer that the machine-gunner concealed in the brush to his right flank wouldn't hoof it. That would be the end. He forgot the tank and his men for a moment. Bending down he fumbled with the two mines at the bottom of his pit, checking the fuses once more, lifting them to test their weight, wondering how fast he would be able to run with them.

His thoughts were shattered by the scream of horror in the next hole. He flung up his head. The Tiger had stopped. Now it was screwing to left and right some 300 metres to their front.

Vassily swallowed hard, eyes filled with animal horror. It was the pit occupied by the forward observer. A rat called simply the Old Soldier because he often boasted he had been in the army since the Russo-Japanese War of 1905, had volunteered to man the observer post. Now he had been too slow to make his escape.

Next to Vassily, the man who had screamed did so once more in a kind of eerie inhuman manner, his head thrown back to expose a scrawny unshaven throat like some moon-crazed animal baying at the unknown. Vassily knew why. The man was visualizing what was happening in that hole, as the Tiger ground back and forth, trying to break in the sides with its tracks until its whole weight could fall on that lone old man. For one long moment Vassily visualized it too: all light blacked out by that tremendous metal bulk, the overpowering stench of fuel, the ear-splitting roar of great motors, the terror of the old man as he held up his hands trying to ward off his fate pathetically, his trousers filled with piss and shit, and screaming, screaming, screaming silently... 'They're coming on, comrade captain!' someone yelled.

The Tiger had done its murderous work. The Old Soldier lay crushed to bloody pulp at the bottom of the shattered trench. The tank was advancing purposefully once more, the crouching SS men following it in a tight cluster. Vassily flashed an anxious glance to the bushes on his right. The Tiger had already clattered past. Now the Fritzes were parallel with the hidden machine-gunner. Would he dare open up now after he had seen, too, what had happened to the Old Soldier? Vassily felt his hands clench to sweating fists, the nails digging deep into his palms. Was the swine never going to open up?

Suddenly there came the hoarse slow chatter of the old '05 model Russian M.G. like the angry pecking of an ancient woodpecker. Behind the tank the SS were galvanized into frantic action like marionettes in the hands of a puppet-master abruptly gone mad. Arms and legs flailing crazily, they were going down everywhere, caught completely by surprise, and at that range the lone gunner could not miss.

Unaware that its protecting infantry was dying behind it, the massive Tiger crawled on. Vassily took a deep, anxious breath. It was now or never. He rose and gripped the two sticky grenades. 'For God's sake, don't anybody fire!' he commanded above the roar of the tracks and engines, surprising himself at just how calm his own voice sounded. 'And stick to your posts!'

He flung himself out of the hole and crouching low, started running towards the steel monster.

The colonel gasped with shock and horror. Instinctively he knew that the running man had to be Vassily. No one else would be bold enough to attempt what he was now trying to do: knock out the Tiger with the pathetic little sticky grenades that he clutched in both hands.

Mouth opened stupidly, he followed the running man's progress as he raced across the shell-pitted ground directly towards the Tiger, hoping against hope that the Tiger's gunner would be caught off guard long enough for Vassily to find a blind spot in the tank's massive bulk.

Two hundred metres … one hundred and fifty metres … one hundred… Man and machine were heading towards each other on a collision course. The colonel felt the sweat trickle cold and unpleasant down the small of his back. It was impossible. Vassily could never pull it off.

Suddenly the Tiger gunner became aware of the running man. Tracer spat from the turret M.G. Vassily zig-zagged violently. He fell.

The colonel gasped.

Vassily was up again and running once more, head tucked deep between his hunched shoulders, white tracer cutting the air all around him, like a man racing through a hailstorm.

Twenty-five metres.

The Tiger ground to a halt. The tank commander was obviously alarmed. Perhaps he had seen the objects Vassily was carrying through his periscope and recognized them? Now the turret gunner swung his weapon round, as if he were taking a very deliberate aim at the running man.

Vassily dived to the ground just in time. The angry burst zapped through the air just above him, ripping open the trunk of a tree behind. Wood splinters, bark and leaves flew everywhere in a thick green rain.

The colonel prayed. Had Vassily been hit?

He hadn't! He was up again before the turret gunner could react. Pelting forward, he spun to the right, outguessing the gunner who swung his weapon to the left, spitting slugs at 800 rounds a minute. Next moment he had vanished from view momentarily. The colonel breathed out hard. He had successfully completed the first phase.

Suddenly the Tiger's driver started to accelerate. The watching man knew why. The commander had ordered him to move off quick before the unknown assailant managed to get on the Tiger's upper deck. Now the battle between man and machine could really commence.

Blinded by flying mud and pebbles, Vassily ran after the monster, his chest threatening to burst at any moment, kept running only by the knowledge that if he didn't make it now, his company, perhaps the whole battalion, would be wiped out. Eyes narrowed to slits against the earthen wake, Vassily searched the Tiger's massive square rear for some handhold. The twin exhausts were nearest. But they were already a glowing purple and he knew one touch and the pipes would sear the flesh off his hands right down to the naked bone. Where else?

Then he saw what he needed. Some careful tanker had placed an extra link of track over the engine cowling, one of the Tiger's weak spots, as additional protection against enemy anti-tank fire. The track link was all the hand-hold he needed.

Summoning up the last of his strength, knowing that in a couple of minutes the racing Tiger engines would draw it away out of his reach, Vassily darted forward, transferring the grenade in his right hand to his left as he did so. He extended the hand. The Tiger was almost within his grasp. He pelted on, the dirt pattering off his bent helmeted head like tropical rain on a tin roof. His outstretched fingers touched metal. He closed them. He felt himself being dragged forward. He hung on grimly. He tugged. His knees smashed against the back of the tank. He heaved and then he was sprawling there on the wildly bucking deck, heart pounding furiously, as if it might explode out of his rib cage.

What seemed an eternity passed while he lay there, all strength gone from his body, save for his left hand, which clasped the two grenades as if they were the Holy Grail itself.

On the bank, the colonel groaned out loud. Vassily had failed! The Tiger was only a hundred metres away from the company line. In a minute it would swing right and then roll up the whole position, grinding each hole to pulp in its turn, making of it a tomb.

To the right of Vassily's entrenched company, a gulag rat popped from his hole, rifle abandoned on the parapet in front of him. Screaming furiously, tearing off his helmet and flinging it away, as if it might hinder his flight, he started to flee to the rear. The rot had set in. In another minute they'd all be running for their lives.

The colonel did not hesitate. 'Gunner,' he commanded to the M.G. gunner to his left, 'shoot that man!'

The gulag rat flashed the colonel a look.

'Kill him, I said!'

The gunner muttered something, but he bent over his weapon all the same. He pressed the trigger. The M.G. chattered. To their front the running man stopped abruptly as if he had run into a brick wall. His hands fanned the air wildly, then his knees buckled under him and he pitched forward on his face, dead.

Vassily heard the chatter of the machine-gun and the scream of mortal agony above the rattle of the tank's tracks. It woke him to the danger of the situation. He got to his knees, eyes searching for the best position to place his grenades. He knew that to the front of the turret would be completely useless; the Tiger was too heavily armoured there. The engine cowling? He dismissed it. The grenades might knock out the engine, but the crew would still be able to use that tremendous gun of theirs. No, not only must he immobilize the Tiger, he must also ensure the gun would not be able to fire.

He had it — the right track and the turret mounting between the turret and body of the Tiger.

Precariously he started to make his way across the swaying deck of the Tiger, holding on the best he could, both hands occupied with the grenades.

Suddenly there was a frantic whirring. They'd heard him down below! The turret started to swing round. Of course they were going to swat him off with the great overhanging cannon just like a horse might attempt to swish away some irritating horse-fly with its tail. He ducked just in time. The 88mm hissed above his head with millimetres to spare. Next instant Vassily slammed home the sticky grenade between the turret and just below the gun mounting. There was a satisfying magnetic clash as metal stuck to metal.

The turret hatch went up. He caught a glimpse of a white face — a hand clutching a pistol trying to find the impertinent swine who was trying to destroy this proud metal monster. Vassily was quicker off the mark. His own pistol barked. There was a thin scream.

The pistol clattered to the deck and the face disappeared. Vassily waited no longer. Leaning over the edge of the Tiger, he held the sticky grenade as close as he dared to the whirring track. The magnetic force virtually dragged the grenade from his hand. It clamped home against the track. A second later, Vassily flung himself over the side of the tank and hit the ground with an impact that knocked all the breath from him.

The first grenade erupted. The Tiger's great cannon dropped like a stone and clanged against the deck with a great echoing slap of metal against metal. An instant later the second one detonated. The Tiger ran on, leaving the track to fall behind it like a severed limb and then its bogies were driving no longer. Slowly, inevitably, it rolled to a stop.

Vassily closed his eyes, all energy drained from his body, as if a tap had been opened, and lay there listening apathetically to the cries of his gulag rats as they streamed forward to slaughter the crew of the helpless monster. He lay there for what seemed an age until one of his rats dropped half a loaf of looted German black bread on to his chest.

'Comrade captain — Fritz grub!' a hoarse, exuberant voice cried. Vassily opened his eyes to stare up at the triumphant gulag rats, one looted loaf stuck on the end of a bloody bayonet, the other held in a dirty paw, his mouth full of bread.

'Thanks,' was all that Captain Vassily could manage to say.

The colonel lowered his glasses with hands that trembled slightly, the image of that shattered Tiger still burning on his mind's eye. They had been saved once again. The gods, seemingly, were still on the side of the gulag rats. He turned and stared at the unshaven, emaciated faces of his men dug in at the side of the river bank. Beyond them the city of Warsaw, clouded as it had been for two days in a thick pall of black smoke, was split here and there by the scarlet flash of artillery fire.

There weren't so many of them left now — perhaps 500 unwounded out of the original 1200-man strong battalion — and the fishermen's cottages down close to the river were packed full with unattended wounded. For forty-eight terrible hours they had held off all that 5th SS Panzer *Viking* could throw at them. But how much longer could they hold on? Just like the embattled Poles on the other side of the Vistula, they seemed to have been abandoned to their fate.

It was over thirty hours since their radio had been knocked out by Fritz artillery fire. Now all they had was an old radio found in one of the cottages. And on it they received nothing but the Polish underground radio station in Warsaw screaming to the world for help — just as they would do, if they could. To Moscow. To London. To Washington. And none was forthcoming.

To the east there was the familiar thick crump of artillery. The Fritzes were going to put in the usual 'hate', now that they knew their own attack had failed. It was time to take cover once more.

'Vulf,' the colonel shouted down to the politcommissar, who sheltered below in the cottages, 'lay on an officers' group for twenty hundred hours — as soon as it's dark!'

'Yes, colonel,' Vulf yelled back as the first shells ripped the August sky apart like the sound of canvas being torn. 'Will do!'

Then the colonel ducked into his grave-like hole and let the full weight of that earth-shaking, terrible bombardment descend upon him and the rest of his rats once again...

CHAPTER 2

Slowly Bor dictated his message to the sweating operator, who tapped it out to London on his morse key, starting every time the cellar shook under the impact of yet another German shell.

'Fighting to retain initiative... Spirit and morale of troops and commanders excellent... People enthusiastically co-operating... Old City and main buildings are in our hands... But enemy beginning to use heavy tanks and are expected to be reinforced by further panzers...'

A particularly heavy shell landed close by. The cellar trembled violently and plaster dust came floating down from the whitewashed ceiling like thin snow.

'Did you get that?' Bor asked the pale-faced operator, telling himself he was only a boy; he had a right to be afraid.

The boy swallowed hard, as if his throat were constricted.

'Yessir,' he said.

'*Dobra*. Let us continue... We are afraid of nothing except that we might run out of ammunition... Therefore' — Bor's voice hardened — 'I categorically demand help in ammunition and anti-tank weapons forthwith! We stake everything on holding the capital. *We must have the weapons!*'

Standing next to him, Brigadier Okulicki bit his bottom lip. He was no longer as confident and as aggressive as he had been four days before. The Home Army had suffered heavy losses and the Fritzes had proved themselves tougher than he had anticipated. 'I would suggest the Jewish Cemetery, Napoleon Square and ... er ... the Little Ghetto as Dropping Zones for the RAF, Bor,' said the brigadier, raising his voice as yet another shell slammed home in the shattered buildings above their head.

'Yes, good,' Bor passed on the information to the operator. 'And let them inform us from London when they're coming. Usual procedure. BBC Polish service to inform us by melody.'

'Sir,' the radio operator said smartly and started tapping out the last of the long message, knowing that each of the dropping zones was identified by its own melody.

Taking the brigadier by the arm, the head of the Home Army walked him out of earshot of the operator. The underground army was full of leaks; he couldn't be too careful.

'Well, what do you think of the general situation Okulicki?'

The brigadier frowned. 'Mixed, like good Polish bacon,' he replied, attempting a little joke, 'partly fat, partly lean. We have no real problems in the Old City, as you know. In fact, I have just heard that the Fritzes are blowing up the last of their bunkers because they can't hold them against our men.'

Bor smiled. 'That indeed is good news. We really have got them on the run then?'

'Yes. That's the fat. Now the lean. I have reliable information that the Fritzes are bringing armour across the Vistula into the capital.'

'But the Russians?'

The brigadier pulled a sour face. 'The Reds are making no attempt to advance, Bor. They're marking time over there, with their rifles at their feet, to use an old soldier's expression. They want the Fritzes to wipe us out before they start advancing again. So, my forecast is that we can expect a Fritz tank attack — a kind of counteroffensive — within the next forty-eight hours.'

'What is the situation with anti-tank weapons? Yesterday only two English bombers managed to get through, I hear. What did we get?'

'Chicken feed! Twelve containers out of the twenty-four dropped and only three of those contained PIATS. In one container there were even bundles of contraceptives,' the brigadier said scornfully. 'As if we wanted to fuck the Fritzes to death!'

Bor gave him a tired smile, telling himself how much the brigadier, who had originally been a puppet of the exile Polish Government in England, had changed in such a short time. Now he was the most bitter critic of the exile government and the British allies. 'What were the Tommies' losses?'

'Five bombers shot down — for twelve containers.'

Bor frowned and slowly wiped some flakes of white from the sleeve of his shabby trench coat. 'They won't keep — I mean the Tommies — they won't keep it up long with those kinds of losses, and we must have those damned anti-tank weapons. This very night if possible.' The brigadier's face hardened suddenly and there was that old aggressive light in his blue eyes. 'Let's shame them into it,' he suggested.

'Shame them?'

'Yes. Let us forget all rules of military security. Let the Fritzes know that we are short of anti-tank weapons. They're going to find out soon enough as it is.'

'And?'

'*A public broadcast*, letting the world know our situation, and how desperately we need the weapons.' Bor's face lit up. 'Ah, I understand, brigadier. There'll be a public outcry. The papers might take it up. Then Churchill's hand will be forced.' Suddenly Bor's smile vanished. 'What if Churchill manages to get our broadcast censored?'

'Impossible, Bor. The neutrals will pick it up too — the Swedes, the Swiss and so on. It'll get to London, if only as a report from "a reliable neutral source". You know the sort of thing?'

'All right,' Bor said, convinced. 'What are we going to say?'

'This.' There was iron in the brigadier's voice now. His face twisted and bitter, he commenced, 'Just as in 1939 Poland was deserted by its Western Allies, Warsaw is again receiving no aid in its desperate struggle against the Germans. We need weapons, weapons, and more weapons. We are not afraid to shed our blood. But what use are bare hands against enemy tanks?' The brigadier's voice rose. '*Send us anti-tank weapons …* *now!*'

Tears started to stream down Bor's cheeks…

'*Donnerwetter!*' *Standartenführer* Kass said triumphantly and handed back the radio intercept to his chief-of-staff. 'It looks as if it's going to be a walkover, Hans. We'll catch the Polacks with their skivvies down! Even my cheeseheads and spaghetti-eaters should be able to deal with them now!'

The chief-of-staff puffed at his cigarette, held in the ivory holder, and stared out of the window at the long line of tanks and armoured personnel carriers crossing the river into the suburbs of the capital. 'It might be a trap, general. A come-on,' he suggested slowly.

'Don't wet your knickers, Hans!' Kass said jovially. 'After all, we are soldiers with armour and basically we're facing armed civilians, who, if we are to take this radio broadcast seriously, lack any kind of anti-tank weapons. What kind of damage can people like that inflict upon SS *Viking*, I ask you?'

The chief-of-staff sniffed, and then turning, stared directly at the *Standartenführer*, all affectation gone from his intelligent face. 'General, they are Poles and they are fighting for their lives.' He clicked to attention. 'Now please excuse me, I must go and prepare — for the slaughter.'

Standartenführer Kass stared at his back, suddenly deflated.

Vulf stared at Vassily expectantly as the voice died away and the ugly, old-fashioned radio in the centre of the fisherman's hut went dead.

But the captain did not react. Instead he stared at his mud-stained boots, as if he were drained of energy.

Vulf gave a little shrug and then, seeing that Vassily did not seem to want to air his knowledge of Polish for reasons known only to himself, did the translation for him, while the assembled officers and senior sergeants listened attentively.

There was silence in the hut after he had finished with his translation broken only by the obscene howl and solid thump of the German mortar barrage outside.

Finally the colonel, his head bandaged now from a slight shrapnel wound, said: 'It looks as if the Polacks over there are pretty much in the same boat as we are.'

One or two of the officers nodded their agreement, too weary to put their thoughts into words.

'All right,' the colonel said, forgetting the Poles and their problems, 'this is the situation. As you all know, we have a fairly good defensive position here on the river — rather like a bite into the bank — with both sides protected from an armoured attack by the thick woods to each flank and the steepness of the terrain closing to the Vistula. The Fritzes are forced into frontal attacks all the time, and under existing conditions, they can do little with their artillery except —'

'Making me shit my pants!' Sergeant Griska interjected coarsely, rubbing his unshaven chin.

The others laughed wearily.

'Yes, except that,' the colonel agreed, telling himself that the gulag rats' spirits were not altogether broken yet. 'However, today the Fritzes came with a tank and it was only thanks to Captain Vassily that we managed to hold them.'

Vassily looked at his feet.

'My guess is,' the colonel continued, 'that they'll try it again, and we can't always rely on having another Vassily on hand to risk his neck like this afternoon.' He paused and let the thought sink in. 'So what are we going to do?'

Under-Lieutenant Donat, a handsome young officer, who had been sent to the Gulag because he had allegedly seduced the daughter of a senior party official named Khruschev in the Ukraine, answered what was really a rhetorical question. 'Comrade colonel, as I don't see what particular function we are serving here except getting our turnips blown off, I suggest we ought to — er — tidy up the line a little.' He grinned, displaying dazzling seducer's teeth below a pencil-slim moustache of the kind the colonel remembered young czarist officers wearing in his youth.

The others grinned too. They knew what 'tidying up the line a little' meant — retreat. After all it was the favourite euphemism of the propagandists back in the Kremlin.

'I'm afraid that is not possible,' the colonel answered.

'Why?' Griska asked.

'I'll tell you,' Vulf beat the colonel. 'Because the only way that a gulag rat can withdraw is on his back on a stretcher — *dead!*' He smiled maliciously, almost feeling the chill which had descended upon the conference at his words.

The colonel nodded sombrely. 'Comrade Vulf is quite right. There can be no retreat for the gulag rats.'

'But if the army commander ordered us back,' Vassily said suddenly with some heat, 'then it would be all right, comrade colonel. Look at it like this. We are about five hundred effectives. About the only food we've got left is what we can take from the Fritz dead. Our ammo is beginning to run out and we can't use the Fritz 9mm stuff in our weapons.' He shrugged passionately. 'What good purpose can we serve if the Fritzes attack all out? Cannon fodder, that is about all we are good for.'

The colonel did not answer immediately. He knew that Vassily was completely right. With the 2nd White Russian Front stalled to his rear, the gulag rats were little better than cannon fodder, waiting like dumb animals to be slaughtered by the Fritzes whenever it suited them. Yet he remembered Rokossovsky's words to him at the beginning of the drive for the Vistula. They needed victory so that one day he, Rokossovsky and like-minded commanders would be in a position to deal with that swine in the Kremlin. He thought a long time, sucking his stainless steel teeth, while the others watched him carefully, knowing that the Old Man was the one who made the decision whether they would live or die in the next forty-eight hours.

The colonel made up his mind. 'All right,' he said finally, 'I shall contact the marshal and leave the decision up to him, whether we stay here and die or withdraw. Our radio is destroyed, as you all know. I request a volunteer to attempt to break through the Fritz line to contact Rokossovsky's HQ.'

As one, his officers and senior sergeants jumped to their feet. The colonel grinned in spite of his inner tension and worries. 'I see you fellers haven't learnt a thing in the Gulag,' he quipped. 'Don't you know that a rat never volunteers for anything —

not even to slip a salami to the politcommissar's pretty daughter?' He shot a glance at Donat.

The young officer blushed and the others laughed.

'All right, Donat, you will go ... Griska, you hairy-assed bugger, you'll go with him. One of the two is bound to get through.'

Griska rubbed his unshaven chin. 'The Fritz who can catch Mrs Griska's handsome son has yet to be born, comrade colonel,' he boasted. 'The NKVD had to put in an Olympic runner to pull me in in 1940.'

The others laughed.

'Well, we'll see, Griska,' the colonel said. 'At least you don't lack confidence.' His face hardened. 'Now this is the message you take to the comrade marshal. Explain our tactical position, naturally, and then say that I expect a full-scale Fritz armoured attack to come in at dawn. It will be an attack that I do not' — he hesitated for a fraction of a second, as if he did not know whether he dared reveal, even to his most trusted officers, the full extent of his fears, 'expect Punishment Battalion 333 to survive.' His glance shot round the circle of suddenly set faces. 'Tell the good comrade marshal that!'

CHAPTER 3

It was dawn, 5 August, 1944.

The skyline across the river was still, silent, broken only by the lazy black smoke rising from the shelling of the night before.

But the colonel's gaze was not directed to the Polish capital. His eyes were fixed on the east, where the sky was already beginning to flush a blood-red, searching the horizon for a sign of movement, his head cocked to one side, ears tensed for the first metallic rattle or hoarse cough of a tank motor having difficulty in starting in the cool dawn air.

Next to him in the dew-wet grass, Vulf whispered. 'Anything, comrade colonel?'

For a moment the Old Man did not react, as if he had not heard the tense question, then he said softly, 'Nothing, Vulf. If the Fritzes are massing out there, they are making a damn good job of it. Not a sound, not even a single fart from some fat Fritz who's eaten too much of that pea soup of theirs.'

'You would have thought —' Vulf stopped abruptly.

'What is it?'

By way of an answer, Vulf indicated the sky to the west.

It was filled with tiny black dots.

'Planes,' the colonel said, suddenly full of hope. 'They look like our Stormoviks, don't they, Vu —' He broke off, the hope draining out of him as abruptly as it had come.

Vulf was shaking his head. 'No, colonel, not our Stormovik dive-bombers. Can't you make out those wings?'

The colonel's heart sank. He could. They were the Fritz Junkers 87s, the notorious Stukas. '*Bosche moi!*' he cursed.

'Tanks are bad enough, but now dive-bombers —' He shook his head and cupping his hands around his mouth yelled, 'Stand to, everywhere! Stand to … *enemy air attack!*'

Frantically the exhausted, mud-stained gulag rats rose up from the pits in which they had slept, fumbling with their weapons, eyes already staring fearfully at the score of hawk-like German bombers, outlined a stark sinister black against the ruddy rays of the rising sun.

'Don't waste any ammo on them!' the colonel bellowed above the roar of many motors. 'You'll need every single round when the Fritz infantry come…'

And then the Stuka squadrons were directly above them. Crouched at the bottom of his own pit, mouth open already to prevent his eardrums being shattered by the blast of their bombs, the colonel could see their black-white crosses quite clearly. Now the shit would begin to fly.

Nothing happened!

To the amazement of the filthy, frightened gulag rats trembling in their holes, the Stukas sailed majestically over the Vistula, dragging their evil black shadows across the silver water, and poised above the city beyond.

For a while they seemed suspended in mid-air like a hawk which had spotted a mouse in a cornfield far below and was preparing to swoop down upon the unsuspecting rodent. Suddenly the leader to the front of the V of planes jiggled his wings, once, twice, three times.

It was a signal.

The next instant the leader's plane dropped out of the sky, sirens howling terrifyingly, hurtling towards the earth at a frightening rate. To the observers on the other side of the river it seemed impossible that the crazy Fritz pilot would ever be able to pull out of that tremendous dive. Then, when it seemed the Stuka must inevitably crash into the city below, the pilot hit the air brakes and jerked back the stick. The Stuka shuddered violently in mid-air and the colonel could have sworn he could hear the screaming protest of the sorely tried metal. A cluster of evil little black eggs streamed down from the plane's obscene, blue-grey belly.

In an instant the buildings below were submerged with smoke. Now plane after plane hurtled downwards, following the leader to discharge its bombs on the defenceless Poles below.

Breathing out hard, the colonel told himself the gulag rats were out of danger for the present.

It was not the rats who were going to be the target of the all-out Fritz attack; it was the Polacks of the Home Army who were destined to be the cannon fodder this particular August morning.

The alarming reports started to flash into the HQ from all parts of the Old City. Everywhere the telephone operators passed on their terrible news while sweating, harassed staff officers sketched in the damage on their situation maps. *'Jerusalem Avenue near river blocked… Fifty dead and wounded outside the Post Office… Attack Force Ghetto buried alive…'*

Bor bit his bottom lip as the blue marks indicating incidents spread like an evil rash across the big wall map of the city. One did not need to be clairvoyant to know that this was the all-out German effort, he told himself. First the aerial bombardment to disrupt the underground army's communications and send the civilians fleeing from the Old Town for the suburbs, thus creating more confusion within the Polish lines, and then the tank-infantry attack would come in.

By mid-morning the Stukas had completed their evil work and everywhere the dazed, deafened survivors stood by their posts in the bomb-shattered, smoking streets, trying to build up their barricades once more before the Germans came.

But the enemy was not yet ready.

At exactly twelve o'clock a sound cut the heavy brooding stillness that lay over Warsaw, the likes of which the Warsawers had never heard before in five years of war. It started in the far, far distance, a dull groaning noise. Startled, the defenders swung their heads to the west. Bright red flashes sparked like the fire that comes from some great steel furnace. Once, twice, three times. The low groan became a scream, a scream which grew louder and louder, accompanied by a high-pitched piercing wind-noise. And then with elemental terrifying fury it was upon them. *One ... two ... three...* The three one-ton shells fired from ten kilometres smashed into the centre of the Polish defences, bursting with a mighty antiphonal crash.

Buildings, bodies flew everywhere. Abruptly the shattered gutters ran with bright-red blood and the wounded were lying everywhere, writhing in agony, crying out for help.

For two interminable hours that savage bombardment continued. Crazed men and women ran back and forth, dodging the masonry which showered down upon them on all sides, until finally exhausted and broken-lunged they sat down on the debris-littered pavement and accepted their fate like dumb animals. A convoy of horses in front of Bor's HQ were mown down and died in their cart traces, flayed alive by the fist-sized, whirling steel-splinters, their carts shattered like matchwood.

Now the shelling had merged into one mighty cyclonic roar that made the very earth shake under the bodies of those who pressed close to it for protection, their hearts beating like triphammers, their lips trembling, their clothes wet with their own urine, most of them already a little mad.

Abruptly as it had started, that tremendous bombardment ended. For what seemed an age the survivors still lay there, unable to believe that it was over, their ears deafened by the loud, echoing roar of those monstrous shells. But finally they clambered to their feet, weakly patting the dust from their clothes, faces awed, white-eyed and shocked, wondering what was to come next as they stared at their transformed city, a landscape as unfamiliar as the moon.

What now? □

At four that afternoon, the NCOs' whistles shrilled all along the German lines. Everywhere the attackers rose from behind their cover and began to cross their start lines. There were few Germans among them. In all, of the sixteen thousand men whom Stahel was going to employ to crush the Poles, perhaps only three thousand were native Germans. The rest were Ukrainians, Poles, Russians, Latvians, plus the Dutch, the Belgians, the French, the Italians, the Swiss of Kass's Division. But whatever the difference in their nationalities might be, the attackers had one thing in common. They were branded as men who had been rejected by their own societies and knew that there was only one future for them — *kill or be killed!*

That afternoon their main task was to break through the Polish defenders of the Old City and reach the river, thus re-establishing communications with the German troops on both sides of the Vistula.

The men from the *Viking* had been ordered to fight eastwards, parallel to one of Warsaw's major streets, Jerusalem Avenue, heading for the Vistula. Kass didn't like the assignment very much. As he confided to his chief-of-staff, 'Hans, it's all right for that pomaded rear echelon stallion,

Stahel. He doesn't have to get his arse shot off. But I don't like risking my tanks in those back streets. A couple of Polacks with a handful of Molotov cocktails could make a nasty mess of my tankers.'

For once the elegant chief-of-staff had agreed with his boss and made a suggestion of his own, 'Let Dirlewanger's poachers do the job for you, general. It's not going to be any great loss for the world if that pervert's criminals go hop.'

Kass had nodded his agreement. He knew all about 'General' Dirlewanger. Before the war he had been booted out of the SS for sexually assaulting a minor and been sent to a concentration camp, only avoiding the death sentence because he had friends in high places in the SS. In '41 Himmler had had him brought out of the camps in order to recruit a special force of SS anti-partisan fighters, made up of imprisoned poachers, who Himmler thought would be the best types for that kind of warfare. The poachers were all long dead, but Dirlewanger had established a fearsome reputation as the most brutal anti-partisan hunter in the whole of the SS. Now the terribly emaciated pervert with his swarthy, skull-like face, led a band of killers, recruited from the SS prison camps, who knew no mercy. Men, women or children, Dirlewanger's criminals killed them all without a moment's hesitation. Thus it was that *SS Oberführer*, Dirlewanger's killers, led the attack of the *Viking* that afternoon, burning a path of terror in front of the tanks, leaving behind them a trail of death and destruction.

The refugee column, mostly women and children, heavily laden with cloth bundles and bursting cardboard suitcases, shuffled towards the Polish barricade, blocking the avenue from one side to the other. Some wept. Others beat their heads with clenched fists, as if demented. A few stumbled on, eyes blank, seeing nothing, hearing nothing, as if they were already mad.

The young Polish lieutenant stared at them open mouthed. If they were not stopped in a minute they would sweep away his barricade. He flashed a glance at the faces of his men, crouched there with their rifles and Molotov cocktails at the ready. They were as bewildered as he was. For what seemed a long time he was too astonished to do anything. Finally he reacted.

Springing on top of the barricade, ignoring the danger presented by the Fritz snipers entrenched in the upper storeys of the houses further up the avenue, he cried, 'People ... people ... go back!' He extended his arms like Jesus on the cross, as if preparing to stop them personally. 'Go back!'

The column shuffled on.

He flashed them a desperate look. What was terrifying them thus? Why didn't they stop? A few seconds more and they would crash into his barricade. □

'*Go back! I say —*'

His words ended in a scream, as the machine-gun burst caught him fully in the chest, sending him flying to the ground.

Next moment Dirlewanger's killers were cutting their way through the screaming women and children, trampling babies underfoot as they smashed into the Polish barricade, their approach hidden by the Poles...

The fat Polish priest started to scream. It had taken the Dirlewangers a long time to find a hammer and nails in the mess of the smoking, shattered church, around which lay the sprawled bodies of twenty dead comrades. But at last they had, and now they were going to have their fun with this fat priest, the last survivor of the handful of Polacks who had caused them so many casualties.

'Up with him!' a drunken sergeant ordered, switching his cigar from one side of his thick-lipped mouth to the other. 'Up with the fat pope!'

A dozen willing pairs of hands propped the screaming priest against the door, stretching out his arms to left and right.

'Hold him straight, for God's sake!' the sergeant commanded angrily and pulled the hammer out of his grenade-laden belt.

Someone held the big steel nail against the priest's right wrist.

In spite of his drunkenness, the sergeant's aim was good. The hammer flashed and the nail sank deep through the flesh and into the wood.

The priest screamed shrilly.

The drunken sergeant threw back his head and guffawed. 'Listen to him, comrades, he's saying his prayers,' he exclaimed. 'Can't yer hear him?'

He pressed his brutal unshaven face closer to the priest's ashen one, 'Why, yer should be grateful to me, pope,' he said tauntingly. 'After all we're making yer a little closer to yer beloved Jesus, ain't we?'

Next instant he raised his hammer and in one quick blow sank the other nail in.

Like a taut bow-string the priest's spine arched and then mercifully he fell unconscious, his head slumping to his chest. That seemed to take the pleasure out of the self-imposed task for the Dirlewangers. Hastily they nailed the unconscious man's feet to the door and hurried back to the fighting.

Left there nailed to his own church door like some fat black crow, a pathetic parody of the crucifixion of his Master, the priest died slowly.

'*Dossvidanya, tovaritsch!*' the bearded lieutenant said and lit the stick of dynamite with the cigar that was glued to his bottom lip.

'*No, no, no!*' the prisoners, stripped naked for the most part, screamed at the bottom of the dry well.

The lieutenant grinned and dropped the spluttering stick of dynamite over the small retaining wall. He ducked hastily. Bits and pieces of human bodies came flying out of the well in a gush of hot steaming blood.

A head rolled to a stop at his feet.

The bearded lieutenant started dribbling it down the debris-littered street, followed by an excited, shouting pack of Dirlewangers. Finally the lieutenant grew tired of his little game. With a tremendous kick, he set the severed head whizzing through the air to smash through the surviving pane of glass in a window at the end of the street. □

'*Goal!*' his men yelled in admiration.

The lieutenant raised his clasped hands above his head in triumph. 'Everyone a winner, men!' he proclaimed.

Thus the Dirlewangers cut their way across the city towards the Vistula, with behind them Kass's Tigers crawling cautiously through the smoking streets littered with the corpses of the Poles that the Dirlewangers had slaughtered.

By nightfall the *Viking* gunners were beginning to pump 88mm shells at Bor's HQ in the Kamler tobacco factory. Bor's staff started to take casualties. Bor gave in to pressure from his staff. He ordered that his headquarters should be evacuated to a school in the Barakowa Street, located in the Old Town.

Here on the roof of the newly captured building, General Kass and his chief-of-staff stared down at the burning city and took stock of the day's fighting, each man preoccupied with his own thoughts, considering the terrible events of the last six hours. It was Kass himself who finally broke the two men's brooding silence. Kass was not a sensitive man. After all he had been a frontline SS officer since 1939, but the happenings of this August day had shocked even this hardened soldier. 'Hans,' he said slowly, almost ponderously, 'if we lose this war, God help us. The retribution for this day will be terrible.'

Solemnly the chief-of-staff nodded his agreement and stared at the leaping flames, as if they were those of hell itself.

CHAPTER 4

'Go on, sergeant,' the marshal said encouragingly, pouring a fresh mug of tea from the bubbling *samovar*, adding a generous slug of pepper vodka, and handing the mixture to the dirty, ragged Sergeant Griska.

'Well, comrade marshal,' Griska said, taking a grateful sip of the steaming tea, 'we'd just got clear of our own positions when we ran into the Fritzes. Foot-sloggers.'

'No armour?'

'No, comrade, just ordinary stubble-hoppers. As far as I could make out, second-line stuff. Old boys for the most part and thin on the ground. Hard luck for Lieutenant Donat though. He wasn't as quick off the mark as old Griska. He took a burst right in his handsome mug — excuse me, comrade — face.'

The marshal smiled faintly. In spite of his own fastidious habits and manner, he enjoyed the tough talk of the common soldier. 'Don't apologize, sergeant. I don't shit through my ribs either you know, although I'm a marshal of the Soviet Union.'

Griska grinned wearily and glanced at the plump pigeon in the corner, filing her red-painted nails and masquerading as a captain in the Red Army. 'Don't look like it, comrade marshal,' he grinned and then deciding not to push his luck too far, continued with his account of his escape from the gulag rats' position on the river. 'Anyway the poor officer bought it and then I was running as if I was trying to win the Olympics and those old Fritz codgers were banging away at me for all they were worth. But fortunately for me, they weren't winning any prizes and about ten minutes later I was nice and snug, tucked away in a thick wood, trying to catch me breath. Yes, comrade marshal, I wouldn't say no to another cup. More vodka this time. My chest is a bit tight still from all that running, you see, comrade.'

The Marshal grinned and winked at the bored girl. 'Thus our common Russian soldier, captain. Vodka is more precious than life.'

The girl sniffed and didn't even pause filing her nails.

'Well, comrade marshal,' Griska continued, 'I walked the rest of the night and about six this morning I sneaked through their lines facing your army.' He took a deep gulp of his drink and gave a belch of satisfaction. 'It was easy.'

'Are their lines so thinly held?' the marshal asked.

'Yes, comrade. A blind man could find his way through them without being caught.'

'*Horoscho*!' The marshal said, business-like now, rising to his feet.

Griska gulped down the rest of his drink as if the mug might well be taken from him before he could finish its contents.

'You have done well. Your colonel should be proud of you. You may go. Tell the big staff captain outside to find you a bunk and that you are to be allowed to sleep undisturbed as long as you wish.' He smiled suddenly. 'If you wish for some plump pigeon to keep you company in the hay, he is to provide you with one.'

Griska's little eyes glittered greedily in spite of his tiredness. 'It's been so long, comrade marshal, that I've almost forgotten.'

'But not altogether?'

'No, comrade. I could never get *that* forgetful.' And with that Sergeant Griska saluted and was gone in a very great hurry indeed.

Rokossovsky turned and stared thoughtfully out of the window, his clever eyes set on the far distance, considering something very seriously.

Konstantin Rokossovsky was a complicated man. Clever, ambitious, militarily talented, ruthless, he was above all vain, exceedingly vain. Vanity had been one of the motivating forces of his life, making him want to outdo all his contemporaries ever since his days as a young officer in the czarist army. It had made him do foolish things but also tremendously brave ones too; for he had an overwhelming desire to shine in the eyes of his beholders.

And it had been his vanity more than anything else which had been hurt that terrible day in late 1938 when the NKVD had come to arrest him: two burly sergeants, one of whom could not even write, to take him, a marshal of the Soviet Union to the Gulag. What had happened thereafter in those terrible months in the camps, where he had been forced to work like a common labourer, dressed in rags, at the beck and call of some illiterate peasant guard, had left him with a burning hatred of the man who had done this to him — Josef Stalin. Admittedly he was still afraid of Old Leather Face, but as the years passed and his own power grew with each new victory, he was becoming increasingly inclined to take risks in order to attain his revenge.

Now mulling over Sergeant Griska's report, he began to discount Stalin's order to him. His old comrade, the colonel, should be supported. There was the start of a vitally important bridgehead on the Vistula which he was not prepared to abandon. But how could he help the gulag rats without Stalin knowing — and he was realist enough to know that Old Leather Face had his spies at every major headquarters, who kept him well informed of what his marshals were up to. *How?*

Then he had it.

Ten minutes later he was standing in the door of the big barn which held the anti-Russian partisans, wrinkling his nose at the stink that met him there. He nodded to the sergeant in charge. 'Bring them outside. I can't stand the stench in here.'

'Yes, comrade marshal.'

They brought the two of them out, hands tied cruelly behind their backs, the nooses which would be used to hang them publicly around their necks. The sergeant shoved them in front of the elegant officer standing there in the middle of the dusty cobbled farmyard, puffing broodingly at his long cigarette.

'Move back,' the marshal said, 'I wish to speak to them alone.'

'They're dangerous, comrade marshal,' the sergeant said hesitantly.

The marshal clapped his hand to his pistol holster. 'Even at my great age, I think I am capable of tackling two unarmed, bound men, sergeant.'

The NCO flushed and indicated that his men should move away.

The marshal waited until they did so, mustering the two sullen Ukrainians who had been taken the day before in a running fight with one of his infantry battalions. 'Which of you is the so-called Gorilla?' he asked and then added quickly. 'You, I suppose, with that hairy mug, you could be no one else.'

In spite of his broken and blackened left eye, the result of a routine beating after he had been taken, the Gorilla spat in the dust next to the marshal's gleaming boots.

Rokossovsky sniffed. 'Pleasant little manners you have, Gorilla. And you, what is your name?'

'They call me Eugen, comrade marshal,' the other prisoner said, his face downcast.

'Hm,' the marshal grunted, telling himself that this was the one he needed. He could be manipulated. 'You two rogues know what is awaiting you, I'm sure?'

'Get it over with, Russian. Don't just chatter on like an old *babushka* with the wind up her drawers,' the Gorilla snarled.

The marshal kept his temper with some difficulty. In the old days when he had been a hot-tempered young officer he would have had a *kulak* like that beaten to death with his knout. 'But you don't have to die, if you don't wish to,' he said softly.

Even the Gorilla was surprised. 'What did you say?'

'You heard me!' □

'What do we have to do, comrade marshal?' Eugen asked eagerly, a new light in his eyes.

'You know this area well, don't you?' the marshal said.

'Yes, we've shit all the way between Minsk and Warsaw more than once,' the Gorilla replied coarsely. 'Why?'

'I have a small group of my soldiers cut off on this side of the Vistula opposite Warsaw.' The marshal hesitated no longer. If things didn't work out as he planned, who would believe the words of two traitors who were bandits to boot? 'I want to ensure that those men receive supplies of food and ammunition. I thought that you and what is left of your men would be the kind of people who would be able to slip through the Fritzes' lines and take them those supplies.'

'As easy as falling off a log,' the Gorilla said. 'The Fritzes have no nose for that kind of thing.' He looked cunningly at the elegant officer. 'How do you know we won't just take off once you've let us go?'

'Easy,' Marshal Rokossovsky said. 'Because *you* won't be going. *You* are going to stay behind as a hostage for the good behaviour of your bandits.' He looked at Eugen, knowing that the other Ukrainian would carry out his orders. 'I am having the supplies loaded in local *panje* wagons so that you will be taken for Polack peasants. You will set off tonight. I have a sergeant from the trapped unit who will guide you to it. Well, will you do it?'

Tears of gratitude filled Eugen's eyes. They were saved. 'Of course, of course, comrade marshal!' He bent, and before the marshal could stop him, he had kissed his hand.

Next to him the Gorilla farted contemptuously, but there was no disguising the sudden relief in his one good eye.

Thoughtfully the marshal walked back to his waiting staff car, wiping the traces of the bandit's lips from his hand with his scented lace handkerchief. Now he was committed. Once again he had gone against the wishes of that monster in the Kremlin.

He said a prayer and got into the staff car, wondering suddenly how it was all going to end.

CHAPTER 5

After a week of fighting, a bizarre way of life had developed in the Polish line of barricades and strong-points, wedged everywhere now by German salients.

Grenades flew back and forth and machine-guns rattled, attacks and counter-attacks were launched throughout the daylight hours; one air-raid followed another so that the defenders' nerves were taut and stretched from dawn to dusk until the short summer nights brought a few hours of peace.

Every house in the line became a strongpoint, with the civilians and the soldiers sharing life — and death — together, praying each dawn at the home-made altars which had sprung up everywhere. Then they would go out for another day's battle just as workmen had set off for the factories before the war.

Parallel with the life in the strongpoints, a strange underground existence took place too. 'Pigeons', as the girl snipers were called, moved from one strongpoint to another by means of the ancient sewers which ran everywhere beneath the capital, popping up to take a quick aim at some unsuspecting German soldier before disappearing down the nearest manhole cover.

But the sewers were used not only by the girl snipers, hunting Germans. As the enemy pressure grew ever fiercer and it was no longer safe to venture into the streets during daylight hours, the sewer system became the main means of communication and transport between the various Polish Home Army commands.

Civilian volunteers, men, women and children, toiled through the stinking, evil tunnels, knee-deep in human excrement, dragging food and ammunition for hours on end. Boy scouts carried messages from one HQ to another, subjecting themselves to the gas that collected in the sewers, and had to be revived at their destination with pure oxygen from cylinders kept there for that purpose. Even small factories were started in the large sewers, where nimble-fingered women and children made hand grenades, filling captured German high explosive into empty food cans and biscuit tins.

It was not surprising that a hard-pressed Bor, fighting desperately an enemy who seemed to be exerting his full weight along the whole length of the Polish line, came to rely more and more on the men and women who now bore the proud title of *Kanalarki*. The *Kanalarki*, deathly pale and smelling to high heaven, were those Poles who could find their way blindfolded through the intricate sewer system, able to spend days below ground, daring to come up behind the German front to surprise small enemy units and gather the information that Bor needed urgently. At first the *Kanalarki* had not been welcome guests at the Bor HQ; now they were honoured there as the bravest of the brave.

Thus it was that the *Kanalarki* brought the news that the Dirlewangers were preparing for a major attack to capture two Polish strongpoints, the Old Arsenal and the main Post Office. Bor's resources were limited, but he knew the Dirlewangers, the most feared of the enemy attackers, had to be taught a lesson before they swept all before them.

'We shall take them by surprise here at the telephone exchange near the Post Office. I doubt whether our brave people can hold out very long if those bandits launch a full-scale attack with tanks on the two strongpoints. But I *do* know that those Dirlewanger criminals will not be expecting us to react so quickly.'

'More than likely they'll be drunk,' replied the brigadier, who, after a week of fighting had become strangely shrunken and laconic. 'They always are after an attack.'

'Hopefully,' Bor said. 'But those pigs *must* be taught a lesson. Don't put it in writing, brigadier, but tell the commander of the *Kanalarki* group that no, I repeat, *no* prisoners will be taken.'

'I will see to it, Bor. And when?'

'Tonight, as soon as it is dark.'

That afternoon, supported by Kass's tanks, the Dirlewangers took the Old Arsenal as Bor had predicted. As usual they took no prisoners. The cellars in which some of the Poles still held out were flooded with gasoline, and a flaming torch thrown into the fuel.

It went up immediately in a great puff of violent orange flame, turning it immediately into a white-hot inferno, in which the screaming, hysterical Poles were fried alive, while the Dirlewangers laughed uproariously, doubled up with joy, slapping each other on the back, holding their noses, and crying: 'By God, don't those Polacks stink! Worse than fresh horseshit!'

Burning, looting, slaughtering, the Dirlewangers advanced on the Post Office and took it too. The male defenders were killed first, many of them being simply tossed off the roof to the street far below, then the boys and women were slaughtered too.

It was in the midst of this drunken orgy at the Post Office that General Kass and his chief-of-staff drove up to talk to Dirlewanger about the situation.

As hardened as he was, Kass nearly vomited at the sight of the mutilated bodies lying everywhere. 'God in heaven, Hans,' he said thickly, mouth full of green bile, 'how can a German officer allow such things to happen?'

The chief-of-staff took his eyes off a dead boy, his short trousers pulled down about his ankles, making it all too clear what had happened to him before mercifully he had been put out of his misery. 'Dirlewanger is not a human being, *Standartenführer*. He is a sadistic animal.' They shoved their way through drunken Dirlewanger troopers who filled the entrance and who snarled back at the two senior officers until finally an enraged Kass drew his pistol and, firing a single shot into the ceiling, cried: 'One more of you pigs gets in my way and I'll spill his guts all over the floor! *By God*, I swear I will!'

The threat had its effect and in a few moments the two SS officers were facing the dark-haired sadist who, as usual, was accompanied by his current favourite disguised as an 'adjutant', a thin, blond-haired teenage officer, whose lips, an enraged Kass could have sworn, were painted.

Kass neither accepted Dirlewanger's outstretched hand, nor replied to his greeting. He got down to business at once. 'Dirlewanger, your command is a disgrace. Your men might be brave, but they are a terrible bunch of drunken hooligans! What would happen now if the Poles counter-attacked?'

Dirlewanger as always spoke of himself in the third person. 'Dirlewanger's honest fellows are a little bit careless in respect of military discipline, general.' He smiled winningly at the red-faced Kass. 'But Dirlewanger confidently believes that the Polacks are so shit-scared of his brave chaps that they run for their very lives at the mere mention of his name.'

'I doubt it strongly,' Kass snorted and felt a sense of nausea as Dirlewanger stroked the 'adjutant's' lily-white hand with one of his own claw-like hands. 'Most strongly. I am ordering you to get your command into shape. Furthermore I am ordering you to improve your discipline. This cannot go on. If it does, I shall have to report your command and yourself to Reichsführer SS.'

'Himmler?' Dirlewanger touched his fingers to his cruel, thin lips, and kissed them. 'Himmler and Dirlewanger are like that. *Sugar!*' Suddenly the smile vanished from his skull-like face. 'Dirlewanger is a law to himself, general. Dirlewanger does what he likes. Dirlewanger takes orders from no one — from neither you nor Himmler. Not even from the Führer himself!'

Kass gave up. He shrugged. 'All right, Dirlewanger, be it on your own head if the Poles attack you.'

Dirlewanger's smile returned. 'No one *attacks* Dirlewanger,' he said confidently, stroking the boy's hand. 'Dirlewanger *does* the attacking.'

Outside an exasperated Kass mopped his sweat-soaked brow, his face crimson with rage. 'The man's mad, completely out of his mind!'

'The man should not be allowed to live,' the chief-of-staff said deliberately. 'Let us hope the Polacks do the job for us.' He looked directly at an angry Kass. 'Otherwise, *mein lieber general*, we will have to do it ourselves.'

The *Kanalarki* attack on the Telephone Exchange that night was a complete success. The Dirlewangers were caught off guard; even their sentries were drunk. The *Kanalarki* slaughtered the Dirlewangers where they lay, drunk in their own vomit, bayoneting them as they rutted with their women on the floor, and then shot the women too.

They took a terrible revenge. No one was allowed to surrender, even when the more sober prisoners went down on their knees and begged the Poles, who stank of the sewers, kissing their excrement-heavy boots in abject supplication. Like the rest they were bayoneted and then thrown from the roof to slam into the cobbles below, every bone in their bodies smashed.

Within the hour it was all over, with the total Dirlewanger garrison slaughtered, the courtyard and the office floors littered with their dead. Swiftly and silently, like the grey sewer rats they had become in these last terrible days, the *Kanalarki* slunk back into the shadows.

Dirlewanger took a terrible revenge. For some time he had suspected that the Polacks had the ability to move secretly behind his lines. Now he knew how it was done, he set about clearing the sewers with the most terrible weapon available to the attackers, the *taifunsystem*, the top-secret system which arrived at his HQ. On that same day he reported to Himmler that he had lost one third of his effectives in the attack on the 'Polack bandits' and was told he would be awarded the coveted Knight's Cross of the Iron Cross for his 'outstanding services to the cause'.

The engineer in charge wanted to explain the running of the *taifunsystem* to Dirlewanger, but the killer, too angry even to be appeased by the knowledge that he had at last been awarded the coveted 'bit of tin' to cure 'his throat ache', snapped: 'Dirlewanger doesn't want to know about your damned toy! Set it up and root out those damn sewer rats for Dirlewanger.'

Embarrassed and not a little afraid of the walking skeleton, whose sadistic reputation had now even penetrated back to the Reich, the engineer hurried to comply. Choosing some twenty of Dirlewanger's 'poachers' who were not too drunk, he wired up a series of manholes covering the sewer system in the centre of the city, then for two hours made the poachers pump explosive gas into the sealed off sewers.

At three o'clock that afternoon he was ready. Dirlewanger finished the experiment personally. Thrusting by the perspiring engineer and kicking a drunken Dirlewanger who was too slow to get out of his way, he snarled, 'Now Dirlewanger will see how those Polack rats will like this!' With that he pressed the plunger that fired the electric sparking system.

There was a bright flash. For a moment nothing happened. Suddenly there was a muffled crump — and another. Immediately to Dirlewanger's front, a manhole cover sailed nearly twenty metres into the air and the ground trembled beneath their feet like a live thing in mortal agony.

The series of explosions seemed to go on forever, proceeding down the sewer system, each one setting off a new one like a jumping cracker until finally the gas gave out and the ground was still again.

Dirlewanger could not wait to see the results produced by the terrible new system. Like an excited child eager to view a long awaited present, he trampled the ground and cried, 'Dirlewanger wants to see... Open up quick!... Dirlewanger wants to see, damn your eyes!'

Hastily the engineer and the Dirlewangers who were helping him donned gas masks and started throwing back the manholes to allow the thick white fumes to escape.

Coughing and retching as if his lungs might be torn apart, but disdaining a mask in his eagerness, Dirlewanger pushed the engineer to one side and peered through the smoke down into the first hole.

The men and women of the Underground Army who had been hiding there had been pulped to jelly by the tremendous gas explosion, their boneless flesh stuck to the sides of the sewer like pieces of meat attached to the inside of a tin.

Dirlewanger chortled with delight. '*Grossartig ... grossartig!*' he exclaimed and clapped his claws together, his skull-like face animated by an unholy joy. 'Dirlewanger wants more ... *more...*'

With the introduction of the *taifunsystem* it became clear to Bor that he had gambled and lost. At first he did not confide his thoughts to his staff, but as the German pressure increased relentlessly and British aid from the air failed to materialize, he knew he must discuss what had to be done next with someone. He picked the brigadier, *the* man who had been the prime mover of the insurrection.

Speaking slowly, as they all did now due to exhaustion and short rations, he explained the position to the silent, attentive brigadier. 'Of course, I know any military force in our present position should surrender, Okulicki, but I can't bring myself to that — yet. I still hope that the Russians will start their offensive again and draw off the Germans. They have that bridgehead still on the other side of the Vistula, don't they?'

The brigadier nodded, but said nothing.

'Morale is high, but the troops are worn out. They need food and they need sleep. I can't give them either. Still we will fight on, but,' he hesitated a moment, 'we must take certain steps to ensure that if we fail, we save the flower of our intelligentsia and our officers for the future. The ones who are the hope of Poland.'

'I will pick them personally, Bor,' Okulicki answered, his tone neutral, though he knew now that the tired, ashen-faced officer sitting opposite him had already conceded defeat: the revolt had failed. 'How shall we get them out?'

'The Russians.'

'*The Russians?*' the brigadier echoed, animation in his voice for the first time for many a day.

'Yes, those Russians on the other side of the Vistula. If they will help us, we can get our men out. Listen…'

CHAPTER 6

The gulag rats, many of them stripped to the waist and enjoying the warm August sunshine, were eating the first real meal they had eaten for many a day — thanks to the Ukrainians and Sergeant Griska — when the high-pitched, hysterical hiss of a Spandau reminded them that there was still a war being fought in Poland.

The colonel dropped his spoon, heaped with salt beef and lentils, back into his mess-tin and stared at the Vistula. From both flanks, tracer was sweeping the surface of the water, zipping in like swarms of angry red hornets. Then he saw the reason for the unusual activity. A small power-boat, occupied by one lone figure was zig-zagging desperately across the river, dodging by a hair's breadth the slugs ripping up the water.

'He'll never do it!' Vulf yelled, rising to his feet.

All the gulag rats along the bank rose too, like spectators at a particularly exciting game of football.

'Of course, he will!' Sergeant Griska bellowed. 'Those Fritzes couldn't hit a barn door at twenty paces. Come on boy! Dodge the bastards!'

Suddenly a groan went through the ranks of the spectators. A burst of fire stitched a line of holes along the length of the rubber-sided boat. The air escaped at once. The motor threshed the water purposelessly. Next instant, the lone occupant was over the side and striking out for the shore in a fast crawl.

The colonel woke up to the unknown man's danger. He was a sitting duck in the water. Already the German gunners were directing their fire at him. 'Get on those guns, you machine-gunners!' he commanded. 'I know you haven't the range. But you might be able to put them off their aim. Come on … there's no time to be wasted!' He flung himself behind the nearest machine-gun and swung it round to the right flank. He knew the old-fashioned '05 model was no match for the Spandau. All the same he pressed the trigger and sent a stream of tracer zipping across the water towards the spot from which the German fire was coming.

In that same moment, Griska and Vassily waded into the water, ignoring the German fire, stretching out their hands to help the young civilian, bleeding from a wound in his shoulder, who was floundering in the shallows.

The colonel's fire had its effect. The German machine-gunner turned his attention to him. Tracer started to whip the bushes all around him. One of the Ukrainians, who was too slow to take cover, screamed and threw up his hands, his chest ripped open by the German fire.

Then the wounded civilian was being dragged up the muddy bank, his blood staining it red, and everywhere the gulag rats were scrambling for cover as the Germans turned the full fury of their fire upon these men who had robbed them of their prey.

Jerzy, for that was the young Pole's name, sat in the command dugout drinking hot tea awkwardly with his left hand, as Vulf completed the bandaging of his wounded shoulder. He muttered a grateful 'spasiva' at regular intervals, but remained otherwise silent, for he knew no Russian.

The others watched him, noting the signs of strain etched by battle on his young, handsome face and the dark circles of hunger and exhaustion under his eyes. The colonel remembered Poles like this one from the old war, when they had nearly captured Warsaw. Their prisoners had looked very much like young Jerzy: haughty, proud, handsome and perhaps a little stupid in their arrogance, but with that unbreakable Polish spirit.

Finally Vulf was finished and said in Polish, 'You wish to speak, Jerzy?'

'*Ja. Ja,*' the Pole said, hurriedly putting down his tea, as if he had just remembered how urgent his mission was to these hard-faced, villainous-looking Russians. Words poured from his cracked lips, so fast that Vulf could not keep up. He threw a quick glance at Vassily, but the captain did not volunteer to interpret. Indeed he was not even looking at the Pole, his gaze fixed on his boots, as if what the man had to say was not of any great importance. Vulf shrugged a little angrily and then said to Jerzy. 'Slow, friend, slow! My Polish isn't that good, you know.'

'*Kak shal*.' Jerzy said in Russian, and then in Polish, 'I shall speak slowly, friend.'

Sticking to simple words and uncomplicated sentences, the young Pole explained just how bad the situation was in Warsaw and how, although their commander, a man known simply as Bor, was prepared to fight on to the death, he wished to save the cream of his young officers and intellectuals.

'How?' the colonel asked as the Pole paused for breath.

The pale young man turned his gaze on the hard-looking officer. 'There is an ancient sewer which runs beneath the Vistula. The Germans know nothing of it. They have plans of the city, but obviously this sewer is not marked on them. So they have not employed this *taifunsystem*. I have told you about against it. That is the escape route that Bor has planned for our people.'

'And what has this escape route to do with us?' the colonel demanded, his face revealing nothing of his inner thoughts.

The Pole hesitated. He knew that to betray the site of the sewer's exit might well mean that the great escape would be doomed to failure right from the start. After all, he was old enough to remember well the great Soviet betrayal of Poland in 1939; he had no illusions about Russian ambitions in Poland. □

'Well?'

'This, sir. The exit is in German-held territory, some half a kilometre from here, and we have not the strength to spring a surprise attack on the Fritzes from within the tunnel. We need help from outside.' He licked his cracked lips. 'Sir, my commander is asking the Russian commander to secure that exit for him.' He looked at the colonel with eyes that were now desperate like those of some hunted animal. 'If you don't help us, the cream of our Polish youth will be exterminated. The Germans will have no mercy on us now.' He reached out his good hand and caught the colonel's arm. 'Sir you *must* help us!'

For a moment the colonel did not move, while the rest of them stared at the scene, the impassioned Pole and the wooden-faced Old Man. Even Vassily had removed his gaze from his boots and was watching the colonel, his eyes full of a strange intensity that seemed almost akin to longing, Vulf could not help but think.

The colonel's mind raced. He held no special brief for the Poles, whatever their political colour. He had fought them more than once and he knew the hatred they felt for Russia; they were no friends of his country and they had only come to him now because there was no other way out of the mess they found themselves in.

Yet they were being slaughtered over there on the other side of the river, not only soldiers, but women and children too. Could the gulag rats sit on their arses in relative peace only a matter of metres away and let it happen — just like that?

He remembered what the marshal had said to him, and Vulf's sinister words on the day they had first reached the Vistula — 'Warsaw must die'. Of course it must in order to satisfy Stalin's territorial ambitions. The colonel bit his lip. If he helped the Poles, he knew it would mean the end of the new career he had built up since he had been released from the Gulag. He would be court-martialled and, if he were lucky, he might escape with his life. Then it would be back to the camps. Could he stand that?

Roughly he shoved the boy's importuning hand away and rose to his feet. Hurriedly the others did the same save the boy, who stared up at him imploringly. 'Will you, *please*?' he asked in a broken voice.

The colonel did not understand the Polish, but he understood the tone all right. '*Ya ne snayu* ... I don't know,' he snapped, almost angrily. 'I just don't know!' And with that he strode away, his hands clasped behind his back, his head bent, as if deep in thought, while the others stared after him in puzzled silence.

'Colonel.'

The Old Man looked up. It was half an hour since the Pole had asked for his aid, and he had still not made up his mind how to answer him. Now he sat in the warm sun apart from the rest of the gulag rats, his handsome face creased in thought, fighting his reason which told him to turn the boy down. 'What have the Polacks got to do with you?' the insidious little voice at the back of his brain kept asking. 'Do you think they'd come running to your help if you were in trouble? Not a chance in hell!'

'Yes, Vassily,' he said, staring up at the young captain, his eyes narrowed against the oblique rays of the afternoon sun, 'What is it?'

'I must talk to you,' Vassily said with unaccustomed nervousness and intensity for him. 'Please, comrade commander.'

'Now?'

'Now!'

'All right, if it's important. Sit down and get it off your chest. But remember that business with the Pole and —'

'It is for that reason — the Pole — that I must speak with you, comrade.'

The colonel looked surprised. 'What has the Pole got to do with you?'

Vassily hesitated for only a fraction of a second. 'Because, sir,' and in his excitement he used the old czarist form of address, 'I am a Pole too!'□

'What?'

'Yes, once I was a Pole too.' He laughed somewhat cynically. 'A Pole, a student, who did not believe in war and violence, and a communist. Now I'm none of those things, simply an officer in the gulag rats!'

'Why are you telling me this, Vassily?' the colonel asked, seeing that the young officer was suffering from considerable strain, as if he might break down at any moment. 'Take your time. I have patience with you.'

'Sir,' again Vassily used the old form of address, instead of the normal 'comrade colonel', as if he deliberately wanted to make the colonel aware that he, Vassily, was not what he had always seemed to be. 'I want you to help that boy over there and the people he represents.' He held up his hand quickly, stopping the colonel from speaking. 'Why, you may ask? I shall tell you, sir. I shall tell you something of my story — and' — Vassily seemed to have difficulty formulating what he had to say next. Finally he got it out. 'What happened at the forest near Katyn...'

CHAPTER 7

'In the summer of 1939, sir, I was twenty years of age, a student of Slavonic languages at the University of Warsaw, which presented no real problems because I came from the border area where we all spoke Russian and Ukrainian as well as we did Polish.' Vassily gave his listener a wan smile. 'Surprisingly enough I was a communist too. Today I can't understand why. I was against the colonels who ran Poland in those days — they were little better than fascists — besides the girl I was sleeping with was a secret party member too. It helped. Sex always does.

'When the Fritzes invaded in September, I thought I might just take a dive and not go to the army. But I suppose I was more of a Polish patriot than I had suspected before. Besides the girl suddenly developed a liking for handsome young officers in uniform regardless of their fascist leanings. So I went with the rest and was posted as a reserve officer to an intelligence unit.'

Again Vassily smiled faintly at the memory of his own naïveté. 'I did not have much of a war, courtesy of the Red Army. We were facing the wrong way when the Russians marched in and after some fourteen days of swaggering around in my new officer's uniform, without ever having fired a shot, I found myself a prisoner-of-war.

'I did not have much time to consider my changed status. With several thousand other Polish officers, I was marched eastwards by the Red Army until we reached the railhead where we were loaded into the *tepluschka*. You know them, sir?'

The colonel nodded. He knew the great purpose-built prison cars, which had existed in Russia since the days of the czar, into which seventy men could be stuffed and locked in for days until they reached the camps.

'At first our *tepluschka* smelt of straw and hay. But not for long. The rotten fish soup which was the only food we were given during our journey soon had its effect. By the time we reached our destination ten of us were dead from exhaustion and dysentery.'

'It has always been the same in Russia, Vassily,' the colonel said. 'The *tepluschka* have always been the means of taking men to their deaths — at the front, or in the camps.'

'Smolensk, our destination, was a relief, even though we were set to road building at once on half rations. Anything was better than those damn rail cars. But the relief didn't last long. Most of the reserve officers were students, like myself, businessmen and civil servants. We were not used to hard physical labour, twelve hours a day, especially when all we had was the most primitive of tools. We started dying, like flies. But I managed to survive, developing a toughness I didn't realize I had.' He smiled, but there was no warmth in his keen blue eyes. 'Perhaps it would have been better if I had died then. Who knows?'

'Go on, Vassily,' the colonel urged.

'Well, when the winter came, we reserve officers, the survivors that is, were taken off the road and placed in a huge camp outside Smolensk. We didn't ask why. All we felt was a sense of relief that we were no longer having to make that damn road and we were undercover before the real snowstorms started.

'Now we were under the command of the police, who, at the beginning, were quite correct. Indeed the first weeks we spent most of our time keeping warm and trying to answer their questions.'

'What kinds of questions, Vassily?'

'A myriad of them and, as always in Russian,' he smiled and added, 'please forgive me for saying so, so damned bureaucratic and confusing that we couldn't figure out their purpose. Later,' his face grew bitter, 'I found out what it was. It was to select those officers who were prepared to cooperate with the authorities.'

'And the rest?'

'The rest were collected together in February 1940, including me. After the camp I was no longer a communist as you can well believe.'

'I know the feeling well,' the colonel said grimly. 'In the Gulag one soon loses one's adherence to the solidarity of the working class and belief in the red future. But go on, what happened then?'

'We were taken into the woods at a place called Katyn, some four thousand of us. Our old guards left and were replaced by the gentlemen of the green cross.'

'The NKVD?'

'Yes, with machine-guns. Silent men who smoked a lot and drank their vodka from bottles they had concealed in the sleeves of their greatcoats when they thought their officers weren't looking. And there wasn't one of them who could look us in the eyes, although we were only ragged, half-starved prisoners and they were the big bosses.' He licked his lips. 'It was then, sir, that I knew I was going to die — that we all were. They were going to kill us with those M.G.s. It was that moment that I suppose comes to all of us when we can foresee clearly our inevitable death — and I didn't want to die! As they set up the machine-guns, fixing the barrels on the mounts, checking the ammo belts and that the water-cooling apparatus was attached correctly — you know, the usual things — I wanted to scream out that I would do anything but die. I was too young to die. I had done nothing wrong. Why should I? But of course, I didn't do a thing. Like the rest I prepared to accept the inevitable, to be slaughtered like a dumb animal.' He paused and looked at the colonel, as if he expected him to say something. But the other man remained silent.

'So there we stood in that freezing wood, feeling that chill in our hearts in the knowledge that in a moment we would cease to exist, that the heart beating so frantically would beat no more, that these eyes would see no more and these hands feel no longer...' Vassily swallowed hard, trying to control the emotion he felt could well overcome him as he recalled that terrible day in the forest at Katyn.

'It all started quite undramatically. There was an order from — oh — a long way off and the first batch of M.G.s started to chatter. We had heard machine-guns firing before, it did not frighten us. None of us were being killed at that moment, and we were so tightly packed together that we could not yet see that our own poor fellows were already being slaughtered in cold blood. And then the firing began to come closer and we could hear the screams, the cries, the pleas, the rattle of the death agony.'

Vassily wiped the sweat from his brow. The colonel stared helplessly at his dirty boots, aware for the first time he was hearing the story of a terrible crime against humanity which had been committed by Russians, by his own people, men who came from the same background and culture as himself, perhaps even men he knew, had served with, had got drunk with and gone to women with in drunken camaraderie.

'Then the mass of officers falling under those constant volleys came towards us like a great, grey wave as they fell, packed so tightly together so that there was no individual falling, just a kind of mass toppling over. It was a gentle kind of end, except for the screams, so that it wasn't even frightening any more — it seemed inevitable, an act of God, against which there was no respite.'

Vassily's voice grew softer and the hectic to and fro of his breast had vanished. 'Then it was our turn and the slugs were flying everywhere. Men were going down on all sides. Something hit me a great whack on the side of the head and I went down with the rest, thinking I'd been fatally wounded, blacking out, my last thought — God, what have I done with my life — *nothing!*'

For what seemed a long time, neither of the two men sitting on the bank in the warm August sunshine said anything, the silence total, save for the muted chatter of a machine-gun on the other side of the Vistula.

'What then?' the colonel asked finally.

Vassily forced a smile. 'Obviously I wasn't dead. I'd been knocked unconscious by a slug which had grazed my right temple.' He indicated the faint scar on his head, which the colonel noticed for the first time. 'But all around me there were the dead, thousands of them. An uncanny feeling, colonel, I can assure you, to awake and find yourself in the darkness with the silent dead all around you.

'Then I heard a noise. It was just light enough to see an NKVD man armed with a pistol, poking around among the dead, and then to his right another one. I didn't need to be a mind-reader to know what they were up to.'

'Checking to see if you were all dead?' the colonel asked grimly.

'Exactly. And almost as if they wanted to let me know what they were up to, there was the sudden single crack of a pistol being fired. They had found some poor swine who was not quite dead. I broke out into a cold sweat, I can tell you, sir. I had escaped death once by some miracle. Now they were coming back to finish me off for good. It was then that I grew angry, terribly angry. I wasn't going to let them get away with it this time. I was going to make a fight for it.'

The colonel could see the small muscles at the side of Vassily's face writhe as he re-lived that moment of determination. 'And?' he asked.

'I wormed my way to the top of the heap of dead and lay there waiting, eyes open, praying that the two NKVD bastards would keep well apart from each other, saying prayers that I thought I'd forgotten years before.' He grinned suddenly. 'They must have helped. At all events I had my man to myself, well out of earshot range of the other one.

'Then he was there, standing on a pile of the dead, staring down at me in the light of the stars. He was quite an old man with dark hair; I can see his face in front of me at this very moment. He had a dark sort of face with slanting eyes, perhaps he was Asian. Well, there he was towering above me, looking around at the bodies, touching this one and that one with the toe of his boot, as if he were checking that they were dead, trying to get a reaction out of some by kicking them a little harder. But there was none, save from me.'

The colonel leaned forward, intrigued now by Vassily's strange story, visualizing him alone among all those dead, with the NKVD man standing there, pistol at the ready. 'What did you do?'

'I groaned. He reacted immediately. He came down from the heap of bodies, fumbling with his pistol. Obviously he thought

I'd be like the rest, easy meat, a Polack pig he could slaughter at his leisure.'

'I let him kneel down at my side and begin feeling for my neck.'

'The neck shot?'

'Yes. He was going to blow the back of my skull off in the usual NKVD fashion. So I let him find the spot and in the same moment he clicked off his safety, I was on him.' Vassily swallowed hard. 'Remember, sir, I was just a callow youth. I had never fired a shot in anger, indeed the last time I had been involved in physical action was a fist fight with a boy in my school when I was twelve. Now I intended to kill a man. It was the law of the jungle — kill or be killed.' He broke off suddenly, his face a mixture of anger and amusement. 'Since then I have killed many men, but that first time I ... it was hard, sir, very hard.'

The colonel patted his arm soothingly. 'I know, boy, I know it well. Forget it. How did you get into the camps?'

Vassily relived that terrible night in the forest, the dead stretching as far as the eye could see, his fingers digging ever deeper into the NKVD man's throat, grunting, *'Die you pig! For God's sake, won't you ever die!'* After an eternity, the NKVD man went limp in his fingers and he was dead. □

'I took the pistol and the man's money and ran, just ran. Ran for an hour, a day, a week, I don't know how long, stealing from the little farms and once, so I think, though I couldn't swear to it, holding up a woman at pistol point and taking the bread she was carrying from her... Then somehow or other, I made myself stop, telling myself, I couldn't keep running for ever. There had to be an end to it, or they would catch me, a Pole on the run with every man's hand against him. *What was I going to do?'*

171

'So you decided the Gulag would be the lesser evil?'

Vassily grinned. 'Yes, sir. There are not many men — at least, those in their right mind — who would take that particular step, but perhaps I was not quite right in the head that February. But it seemed to me the only way out. I couldn't go back to Poland. Someone would have recognized me and denounced me. We Poles have our traitors too. I couldn't keep wandering around the Soviet Union without papers or a pass to move from one place to another. The camps seemed the only answer.'

'How did you do it?'

'Simple. I held up a NKVD post.'

'You what?'

Vassily laughed. 'I held them up and made them make me out a travel pass. Of course, I knew they'd telegraph the next post along the line as soon as I took off and in due course I'd be arrested. Obviously they took me for some idiot who had thrown away his papers in order not to be called up to the army — something of that sort — and was heading for Siberia where he could find a job without papers and where not too many questions were asked. So armed with my new papers, identifying me as Pavel Vassily, I allowed myself to be duly arrested twenty-four hours later. To make a short story even shorter, I got ten years in the Gulag for armed robbery and possession of a pistol. The NKVD magistrate said he was treating me mildly. I could have received the death sentence for having possessed a pistol illegally. I think he took me for a harmless idiot.'□

For a moment the colonel considered Vassily's story, pondered that awful massacre of the Polish officers at Katyn, Vassily alone in Russia, desperately seeking for some means of escape, and was overcome by a sense of desperate longing:

longing for a better world, in which there was a little compassion, just a little.

'Why do you tell me this, Vassily?' he asked coldly, telling himself that there was no compassion on this earth. The intellectuals should toss the very word out of the dictionary; there was no such thing.

'Because, sir, those people over there they are my people — they are Poles! I can't stand by and see them exterminated like those officers were back in '40.'

'Why should I concern myself with Poles? At the beginning of this war they were our enemies and in '20, I fought against them myself, not very far from this spot.' Vassily looked at the harshly handsome colonel with the bitter mouth and the big sabre-scarred hands. Suddenly, for the first time in over a year with the Punishment Battalion, he realized he didn't even know what the other man's name was. For him and the rest of the rats, he was simply 'the colonel' or the 'Old Man'. What did he know about this remote man; why indeed should he help him and those unknown Poles over there?

Desperately Vassily tried to find the words which would convince him, knowing that it was now or never. There would not be another opportunity to gain his full attention as he had now this hot August afternoon. 'Sir, forget that they are Poles. Think of them just as human beings. *Human beings*, sir! Like the people we knew in the camps — in the Gulag. They find themselves in a situation, not of their own creation, but caused by others, who did not ask them if they wanted to be inside Warsaw when the revolt broke out, sir. They were lied to like we gulag rats were lied to. Oh, of course, they knew there was something wrong with the system, after all the Fritzes were occupying their city. So along comes some benefactor,' Vassily's face twisted bitterly, 'there is always such a man in every country, with a plan to change□ everything. Naturally he demanded a sacrifice because one day that sacrifice would be repaid with the universal blessing that the survivors would receive. So they let themselves be deceived by the same old tired words: glory, self-sacrifice, patriotism — what does it matter what they were promised? And now all the promises and big words turn out to be hollow, meaningless, and they are expected to die for those hollow words. But can we let them, sir, I ask you? *Can we?*'

Vassily let the words trail away, all fire gone from his voice, while the colonel rose to his feet and, hands clasped behind his back, walked away from him and stared across the slow-flowing Vistula at the smoke-shrouded Polish capital.

For a moment Vassily was tempted to follow him and continue his harangue; then he decided against it. The colonel wanted to be alone and think the matter over by himself. So he remained there, listening to the soft hum of the summer insects and the lazy tap-tap of the machine-guns on the opposite side of the river.

Once, as a boy, the colonel remembered suddenly, *a propos* of nothing, their cat had produced too many kittens and his mother had ordered him to kill two of them. He hadn't thought much of it. He was a country boy and he was long accustomed to such things. Besides there was nothing attractive about the kittens: they were simply little warm blobs of fur, devoid of any sense, about as important as some blind slug found underneath an upturned log and crushed to death beneath his heel.

But the murder of the first kitten had not been as easy as he had anticipated. At first he had placed the little bundle of blind fur on a log and dropped a heavy stone upon it. It squawked but twisted itself free, dragging one shattered leg behind it. He grabbed it and, with all his strength, threw it against the wall of the barn. The kitten had smashed against the barn but had dropped on all three good legs, still alive, and would have run away if he had not grabbed it just in time. □

In the end he had seized a wooden club and hammered at it, the poor squawking thing, until its very entrails had been squashed out of the bloody ball of fur. Then he had leaned shakily against the wall of the barn and had vomited his guts out, the tears streaming down his young face.

Somehow that memory of an event which he had thought he had long forgotten flooded his mind, reminding him of his situation now. Human emotions were like that damned little kitten of forty years' back. However you attempted to batter them, smash them, tramp them down, they always seemed to survive, even in the hardest of men.

Now, although he knew what would be his fate if he went against the marshal's express order not to help the Poles — there would be no hope for him — he could not repress his feeling of pity. He could not let die those young people, for whom Vassily had pleaded so elegantly, without giving them a chance of escape. He could not be that heartless; then he would be the same as those calculating monsters with ice-water in their veins who ran the Gulag.

Slowly, very slowly, as if propelled by ancient rusty springs, he turned and faced the waiting Vassily.

'Sir —' Vassily began, but stopped when the colonel raised his hand for silence and said simply: 'Tell the Pole we will do it, we gulag rats!'

The die had been cast.

BOOK THREE: *THE ESCAPE*

CHAPTER 1

The colonel wiped the beads of sweat from his forehead and breathed out hard. It was still unbearably hot although the sun had gone down over two hours ago.

'There's going to be a storm,' Vassily said softly, as yet another soldier pushed off from the bank, boots tied round his neck, rifle like a yoke across his shoulders.

'In more ways than one,' Vulf said gloomily, for he had been against the whole operation right from the start.

The colonel said nothing. His mind was concerned with the military risk he was taking. He had thinned out his perimeter so that now each hundred metres of front was covered by one man. In this way he had managed to take some 300 men from his severely battered force for the bold operation he had in mind. But if the Fritzes found out just how thinly his front was held now all hell would break loose. Yet it was the risk he had to take if he were going to help the Poles as he had promised to do.

'Vulf has got the less seriously wounded to fall back upon, colonel, if anything does happen,' Vassily said, as if he were able to read the Old Man's thoughts.

'That bunch of cripples,' Vulf said scornfully. 'Most of them can't even crawl, never mind hold a rifle! If the Fritzes attack, we'll be looking at the turnips from below — it's as simple as that, Vassily.'

Vassily laughed softly and watched as another soldier disappeared into the darkness over the river. 'Don't pull my pisser, Vulf. Politcommissars never go hop. They live on to get fat bellies and join the local state central committee.'

The colonel did not give Vulf a chance to reply. 'Listen Vulf,' he said urgently, 'I know you are not a military man, but you know enough to manage this situation. Just keep the rats in line, don't try to provoke any kind of enemy action. Fire back, if you're fired upon, but that's all.'

'Don't worry, comrade colonel,' Vulf said hastily, 'I'm in no hurry to achieve any kind of military glory. Medals are not much comfort when you're looking up at the turnips from under two metres of earth! Believe me, I'm a devout coward.'

Even the colonel, worried as he was, laughed softly. The little ex-intellectual was honest enough at least. 'You'll manage all right —' he began, but the single, searing, razor-flash of lightning and the instant eruption of thunder drowned the rest of his words.

For that instant the sky above the river was a blinding, brilliant white, revealing heads bobbing in the water everywhere, paddling along or being carried by the slow current towards the north and the suburb of Praga, their objective. The colonel caught his breath as he realized, once again, just how risky this operation was. His men would be in the water some 500 or 600 metres floating — hopefully — past the Fritz positions on the river bank to their front. But what if the Fritzes had dug in all along the river, right into the suburb itself?' He dismissed that impossible thought, and as the sky darkened once more, he reached out his hand to Vulf. 'Do your best, you little rogue,' he said with sudden warmth.

'I'll try,' Vulf answered uncertainly. 'But you shouldn't do this, colonel, you shouldn't!'

The colonel laughed. Next instant he threw his own bundle into the water and waded after it, telling himself that even the river was too damn warm. Vassily followed, watched by Vulf.

But not only the little bespectacled politcommissar was surveying the departure of the gulag rats on the Vistula that night. Hidden in the bushes above Vulf, Eugen, the Ukrainian, took in the scene, his mind racing as he formed the plan that would not only free him, the Gorilla and the rest, but also ensure that they would be able to return to their lost homeland in peace.

The young officers, all of their faces marked by the weeks of fighting, grouped around the map illuminated by the hissing kerosene lantern, as Bor outlined his plan. 'Gentlemen, in the light of the present situation in Warsaw, I am sure that some of you will consider that I am being too bold, perhaps even a little mad. But I am certain you all know, as professional soldiers, what Napoleon said about boldness?'

'*L'audace, toujours l'audace.*' Major Jan quoted the old adage — incorrectly.

Bor nodded. 'Exactly. Surprise will make up for our lack of numbers and weapons. So this is the plan.' Bor tapped the map. 'Major Jan, I want you to take your group and attack from the Bank of Poland into the Bank Square, where you will be joined by *Kanalarki* who will emerge from the sewer manhole there. Together you will continue the advance down the Elektoralna Street to the Zelazna Brama Square.' Bor paused and looked at the battle-hardened officer's faces.

The reaction he saw there was what he had expected and hoped for: surprise and determination.

Major Jan looked at the others. 'God, we'll put the wind up the Fritzes! They won't be expecting us to be coming out of our holes, fighting. It'll be like a shot of vodka for the morale of my boys.'

'There will be a special ration of fifty grammes of spirits for each man,' Bor said.

Next to Jan, his friend, Captain Trzaska, slapped his hand to his forehead in mock amazement. 'Now we can all die happy — *vodka*!' There was a rumble of soft laughter from the others crowding the cellar.

Bor waited till it had died down and then continued. 'You, Captain Trzaska, will get your share of the firewater, too, never fear. I want you to lead your group in a parallel attack from Danilowiczowska Street through Senators' Street and from there through Zabia Street. In this way we hope to split the sizeable German forces in the area, in particular those pigs of the Dirlewanger from the SS tanks.'

The smiles vanished from the officers' faces to be replaced by looks of utter, total hatred. There was not one of them not prepared to sacrifice his own life if he could take a Dirlewanger with him.

'Do we get a crack at the bastards?' Jan asked eagerly. 'Do you know what the swine did at the cellar hospital they captured yesterday? Naturally they raped the girls — they always do. But then they got drunk on medical alcohol and turned their flame-throwers on the wounded as they lay on the floor, helpless as babes in arms!' His young face contorted bitterly. 'They're not human beings, the Dirlewangers, they are savage animals!'

There was a murmur of agreement among the others.

Bor decided this was the best time to end the briefing before the young officers started to ask awkward questions. 'That time will come, gentlemen,' he said as resolutely as he could. 'I have my plans. But for the time being we must be content with baking little rolls. But the time will come.' He clapped the map together with an air of finality.

The officers snapped to attention.

A little wearily Bor touched his two fingers to his bare head in the traditional Polish military greeting. The officers returned it and filed out to begin their own planning.

The brigadier waited till they had all gone before he spoke, his voice devoid of any emotion, even of admiration for the way that Bor had handled the briefing. 'They bought it?'

'Yes,' Bor slumped down suddenly at the packing case table, face supported in his skinny, dirty hands. 'They bought it. It … it is hard to send brave men to their deaths, without being able to tell them the truth.'

Okulicki nodded his understanding. 'It is always hard to send men to their deaths, whatever the reason,' he said with a trace of his old aggressiveness and determination. 'But those of us who survive will remember them and their sacrifice.'

'I suppose so,' Bor said, suddenly very matter-of-fact once more. 'The escapees are ready?'

'Yes, Bor, all six hundred of them. They are ready to enter the sewer immediately the feint attack goes in and occupies the Fritzes' attention. Jerzy will lead them.'

'What of the Russians?'

'Our observers on the river bank report that it *appears* they have left their positions, though of course they can't be certain.'

'Of course,' Bor mopped his dripping brow and cursed the oppressive heat, silently wishing that the storm would break and cool the air. 'Funny isn't it, Okulicki. Here we are, Poles, planning the sacrifice of our fighting men in order that the flower of our youth might escape and relying exclusively on the Russians to help them do so. Do you think we are not making a great mistake, eh?'

The brigadier shook his big, shaven head. 'No, Bor, it is the Reds who are making the mistake, for whatever happens here in Warsaw now, those young men and women will be the hope of Poland.' His voice rose and there was an almost fanatical light in his dark eyes, ringed as they were by the deep circles of exhaustion and strain. 'They will not forget, Bor, nor will they forgive! One day, when the Fritzes have long vanished from our land, driven back across the Elbe from which they came, Poland will rise again. Be it a year, a decade, a hundred years, believe me, Bor, *Poland will rise again...*'

At midnight exactly, Jerzy started to let the young men and women, who were crouched everywhere in the ruins around the square, cross in batches of twenty to where the manhole covers had been removed. To each group he gave the same brief lecture, feeling the beads of sweat dripping unpleasantly down the small of his back and telling himself the sewers below would be like a furnace now. 'There will be four kilometres to cover to the river bank. It must be done in two hours. Anyone who feels unwell or must stop must not hold up the column. Each one of you will hold on to the shoulder of the person in front. No letting go, no stopping. All right, move off!'

One by one the men and women clambered down the dripping ladder into the stinking pit, where the heat and stench of human excrement took their breath away. Jerzy had no mercy upon them. With muttered curses and in some cases swift kicks, he urged them ever downwards, knowing that he had exactly two minutes to clear each batch and another three to let them get accustomed to the glowing darkness and be on their way before the next group assembled above.

By one o'clock he had 500 men and women below ground, a frightened, nauseated human chain, stumbling along in the gloom, sometimes up to their waists in the revolting human sludge, coughing and spluttering, trying to hold their noses with their free hands, drenched by the torrents of water that fell from the bomb-damaged roof at frequent intervals. Now he could tell from the little noises to his front that Jan and Trzaska, the poor bastards who probably wouldn't live to see another dawn, were approaching their start line for the surprise attack on the Fritzes. Time was running out rapidly and he didn't want to be caught above ground when the storm broke. His fugitives would be a sitting target for any German machine-gunner who might catch them in the open by the light of the storm.

He called forward the last three groups, gave them the briefing and said: 'We're going down together. There is no time to be wasted now. Follow me!'

Without waiting for their reaction, he swung himself down into the hole, feeling the stench assail his nostrils like a physical blow. Letting go of the ladder half way up he dropped expertly into the goo, holding his hands up above his head so that he did not have to touch the stuff.

He pushed forward alone the best he could, listening to the hollow sounds of those who had gone before in the dripping tunnel. When he came level with the teenage sentries in their cotton-wadding masks who marked the extent of the Polish perimeter, he stopped. 'Last group coming through now,' he said to their leader, a bespectacled girl, whom he assumed would be quite ugly if she removed her mask.

'When they're through, beat it.'

'Beat it?' she echoed, her voice muffled by the mask.

'You heard me!' he said angrily, knowing these masked figures, soaked to the skin and smelling to high heaven, did not belong to the select group. They were doomed, in spite of their youth, to stay behind and suffer the fate of the rest of the Polish garrison. 'Get back above ground as soon as you can and take a dive.'

'But —' the girl started to protest.

He cut her short savagely, 'There are no more buts. Don't you damn well understand, girl? We've lost! *Now we're running for our lives...!*'

General Kass, stripped to the waist, clad only in his boots and breeches, pressed himself closer to the whirring electric fan, savouring every single cool breath of air. Next to him, the chief-of-staff poured himself yet another glass of champagne from the bottle resting in the ice-bucket. Outside it was deathly still. There was no sound save the steady tread of a sentry. The place might well have been some sleepy, peacetime garrison town, which had not heard a shot fired in anger since the Thirty Years' War.

'*Grosse Kacke am Christbaum!*' the general groaned, 'you would think we were in the shitting tropics and not in Central Europe! It's so damned hot!' He patted his handkerchief against the cheeks of his brick-red, damp face.

'With the general's permission,' the chief-of-staff said, using the old-fashioned third person form of military address, 'the general is inclined to corpulence. It does not help.'

'You mean I'm just too damn fat, Hans,' the *Standartenführer* sighed without rancour. 'I agree. When I'm nervous, I eat, and I'm nervous now.'

The chief-of-staff sipped his champagne and told himself that if his spy had given him false information, causing the two of them to stand by now in the small hours of the morning, he'd have the treacherous Polack bastard strung up by his balls — slowly. 'Why be nervous, general?' he said after a moment. 'We've beaten them. Now it's virtually all over bar the shouting.'

'Is it? Do you think the Polacks will surrender just like that when they find out what the Führer's order is — raze Warsaw to the ground? I doubt it. They'll fight on till the last Polack man, woman — and child too — is dead. There is going to be a blood bath in Warsaw yet, Hans, mark my words.'

The chief-of-staff took another drink of champagne, noting the increased rumbling of the thunder and the sudden flashes of the summer lightning that came through the chinks in the blackout curtains. The storm would break soon; it *had* to. 'Perhaps you are right, general,' he said with a little sigh. 'You know, to change the subject a little, these night-time vigils make me feel philosophical. They always have done ever since I was a young subaltern in the trenches before Verdun in '16.'

'You have always been an elegant shit, Hans. These things have the contrary effect on me. They simply make me damned tired! But get on with it — get it off your chest, if it makes you feel any better.'

'Well, sir, my thoughts are not so easy to formulate.'

'An old regimental commander of mine many years ago gave me this advice, Hans, *stand up, speak up* and *shut up*! That's the way to make a speech.'

The chief-of-staff smiled softly and toyed idly with his glass. 'I was not exactly going to make a speech, general. I was just thinking we've killed the wrong swine, or we've attempted to do so all these years.'

'What do you mean?' The general threw more water at the fan's revolving blades and sighed with pleasure at the momentarily cooled air. 'What shitting swine?'

'The Russian one. When we saw the way the wind was blowing after Stalingrad, we should have made off hell-for-leather for the Reich frontier, leaving nice big dumps of arms for the Ukrainians, the White Russians, the Poles and all the rest of these Slavs, and they would have kept the Popovs occupied for years. All we've been doing since 1943 is to clear the path nice and clean and tidy for the advancing Red Army.'

'You might be right, Hans,' the general said sagely. 'But you tell that to idiots like *Reichsführer* SS Himmler,' he emphasized the title contemptuously. 'The man's a complete fool. Germany bleeds to death and all he can think of is his stupid racial theories. Do you know what he now wants?'

The chief-of-staff shook his head absently.

'That all my officers who want to marry must not only submit a genealogical trace of the bride-to-be's ancestors back to 1760, but also a detailed photograph of the woman so that Himmler's researchers can decide whether her mug, rump, tits and all the rest of the bits and pieces make her Aryan enough to marry one of his beloved SS.' He shook his dripping head. 'The man is mad. *That* in the middle of total war when Germany is fighting for its very life!'

'We Germans are a thorough race.'

'We Germans are fools!' the general snorted. 'And that's why we are losing the war.'

'You have changed your — er, if you will forgive the word? — tune since the start of this Warsaw business. I had the impression a few weeks ago, my dear general, that you still held some faith in the concept of — er — the final victory.'

The general did not answer. Hans, the clever bastard, was right. Now he had lost all hope, but it was not wise to express that particular thought. Instead, he looked straight at the chief-of-staff, posing, as always, with his glass held in his elegant, manicured hand like some pre-war ad for champagne, the heat forgotten for a moment. 'Funny,' he said harshly, 'but in a year from now you and I will be dead!'

It was then that with a great rending crash, the storm broke and the sky fell in. With a tremendous hiss, the sheet of rainwater seemed to drop solidly out of the wildly tormented sky. But even it could not quite drown the sudden snap-and-crackle of small arms' fire.

The general grabbed for his tunic. The chief-of-staff dropped his champagne glass. 'This is it, Hans!' the general chortled gleefully, suddenly happy that the storm had broken at last and he could forget his dire thoughts in fresh action. 'Now we've got a beaut of a battle for you to get your teeth into. *Come on!*'

The last battle had commenced.

CHAPTER 2

On the eastern bank of the Vistula, the false dawn was silent save for the constant drip-drip of the last of the raindrops falling from the trees which lined the promenade leading into Praga.

Carefully, very carefully, the colonel raised himself on the bank, coming up through the low mist which hung over the river like a grey cloak, as if he himself were some kind of water spook, and stared at the dripping trees and the street. The stillness was somehow unnatural, even eerie; but even the wet, clinging greyness could not completely muffle the soft noises that came from the houses at the end of the street. They were occupied all right, he told himself. The question was: were their occupants the Germans?

He made his decision. Bending down, he whispered to Vassily. 'We'll divide into two groups. I'll take one and move down the promenade. You take the other and follow the course of the river bank. We'll link up again at the objective. Remember, you are to avoid combat wherever possible. Our primary aim is to get to that sewer exit and hold it. *Horoscho?*'

'*Horoscho.* But colonel, why don't you let me take the promenade? It's the more dangerous route. I got you into this. If there's any trouble, I should be the one who should cope with it.'

The colonel gave him one of his rare smiles. 'Don't grow sentimental in your old age, Vassily. After all, you are a gulag rat, even if you are a Pole — and gulag rats *never* volunteer. *Davoi!*'

Hurriedly the two officers divided up the wet, shivering men who crouched in the shallows at the bottom of the bank, knowing that every second spent bunched there increased their chances of being discovered by some German patrol.

Five minutes later the two groups were on their way, Vassily's men hugging the narrow path which ran just below the river bank straight into Praga; the colonel's advancing cautiously down both sides of the promenade, using the cover offered by dripping poplars to get ever closer to the first houses.

Now in the dirty white of the new dawn, the colonel, his pistol drawn and at the head of his men, could make out the tall nineteenth-century facades of what once had probably been the villas of prosperous Polish burghers. Now the windows were boarded up and barbed wire draped the somewhat pompous doors, with here and there small defence posts formed with wet, torn sandbags. There was no doubt the places were occupied and civilians did not usually protect themselves with sandbags and barbed wire. The Fritzes were in there all right!

He turned and raised his finger to his lips for complete silence. Grateful for the noise of the gurgling gutters, the gulag rats filed by the first house as silent as grey timber wolves. Once some fool dropped his rifle. It fell to the wet, gleaming cobbles with a noise that sounded to the colonel's startled ears like the crack of doom. He stopped in mid-stride, heart beating crazily, and waited for the first angry shout. But nothing happened. The unseen Fritzes snored on presumably. His hand shaking a little, he gave the signal to continue the advance. The sky was beginning to lighten rapidly, with tattered, luminous-edged clouds scudding by at speed. The colonel increased the pace. Soon it would be completely light. They weren't going to get away with it much longer.

They swung round a corner. To their right was a big building with an open hangar door through which the colonel could see the parked trucks, with the familiar *Wehrmacht* sign on the back. To the left a row of small white-washed cottages. Instinctively the colonel knew that the Fritzes who ran those trucks would be billeted in the cottages; it was standard operating procedure in every army. He jerked his right fist up and down three times — the infantry signal for close up and speed.

The gulag rats needed no urging. The keen morning air was full of the typical stink of Fritz: black tobacco, Fritz hard-soap, and unwashed field-grey uniform. Hardly daring to breathe, each man's eyes fixed on the silent white-washed cottages, his hands clasping his weapon wet with nervous sweat, they filed by on tip-toes.

The colonel successfully passed the last of the cottages and halted, pistol at the ready, watching out for trouble as man after man hurried by him.

Then it happened. A tousled-haired figure in field-grey, his braces dangling down at his hips, a roll of lavatory paper in his hand, came sleepily out of the last cottage, yawning loudly as he did so.

He stopped suddenly, as if he had just run into a brick wall, face frozen in horror, mouth still open in the middle of his yawn, his eyes full of terrified disbelief as he recognized the earth-brown smocks of the Red Army.

The colonel cursed. But it was no use. He raised his pistol and squeezed the trigger. In the same instant that the yell of alarm tore from the surprised German's mouth, the colonel's slug caught him squarely in the chest. His cry ended in a scream of absolute agony and he pitched face-forward into the running gutter, the lavatory paper unrolling itself in a long stream.

In an instant all was confusion and chaos, with rifles barking from every window and the colonel and his rats running for their lives down the maze of small streets that led off from the promenade to their right. The battle had begun...

The 600 young Poles were coming ever closer to the Vistula, wading through the revolting slime, their eyes wild, their faces glazed in sweat. Rats were everywhere, casting enormous shadows on the dripping walls, scampering off in a flash of loathsome long-tailed grey and rustle of claws as soon as the hard-pressed young men and women came into sight.

Jerzy pushed his way by man after man, knocking them angrily out of the way if they were too slow, advancing along the column till he came to its head, where an ancient *Kanalarki*, who stank worse than the sewer, led the group, swinging his hissing carbide lamp to and fro and giving a kind of running commentary on the maze of sewers through which he was taking them, as if he were a peacetime guide running a group of tourists through one of Warsaw's baroque palaces.

Gasping with the effort, his legs trembling as if he had just run a five kilometre race, Jerzy came level with the old man and recognized him. It was the *Kanalarki* whom they called Shit Thomas. He had been a peacetime sewer-worker for the city council and knew the sewer system like the back of his gnarled hand; that's why the *Kanalarki* had recruited him in spite of his age.

'Whores' corner,' the old man croaked, 'that's what we use to call it before the war. Just up there they'd stand on the grating.' His mouth full of rotting yellow teeth, he leered at his gasping young listeners. 'Many's the day I've seen more than I should have done, especially in summer when the whores didn't wear any drawers.' He cackled knowingly.

'Shit Thomas,' Jerzy broke into the old man's lecherous memories, 'how far are we off the Vistula?'

The guide stopped and scratched the back of his shaven head, his lantern swinging back and forth wildly as he did so, casting enormous shadows on the slimy walls. 'Well, there's horse-piss crossing to go. Then stall-shit street. Pissoir-corner...' Maddeningly the old man counted off the places they still had to pass in the jargon of his trade, while Jerzy told himself that now the whole stretch of the sewer would be blocked by suddenly stationary, frightened young people to a length of at least a kilometre.

'Perhaps another thousand metres,' the old fool concluded finally. Jerzy did a rapid calculation. It would take them another half an hour, perhaps even longer, to cover that distance at this pace. Time was running out rapidly. God willing, the Russians would be in Praga now. Their attack on the sewer exit was scheduled to go in at dawn. It was to be expected that the group would emerge at the far end in broad daylight. It was risky, but there was no other way. 'All right, Shit Thomas, let's get going again. I want this lot on the other side of the Vistula by six.'

'Gents like you always want things,' he commented. 'But we humble shit shovellers know things don't always work out the way gents want it.' But in spite of his criticism, the old man continued at once, with an impatient Jerzy now at his side to ensure that he kept up the pace.

Time passed leadenly, the only sound that of the rats and the harsh wheezing of the young Poles' lungs as they stumbled onwards. Now it was increasingly clear that the Fritzes knew of the existence of this particular main sewer. Twice the refugees had to claw their way through a primitive underground barricade of chairs, rations' cases with German lettering on them, timber-beams and rolls of barbed wire which the Fritzes had thrown into the sewer. Jerzy said a silent prayer that the Germans did not know of the existence of the sewer below the Vistula.

Here and there exhausted young people began to drop out. At first their comrades attempted to drag the casualties with them, but not for long. They were virtually at the end of their own strength. They allowed the semi-conscious men and women to sink to the bottom of the sewer, to lie almost gratefully in the revolting sludge, not even looking up as refugee after refugee stepped over them.

A young woman went mad. Suddenly she stopped and started to scream, scream, scream, her head thrown back, with the full power of her lungs. Jerzy felt the small hairs at the nape of his neck stand up erect with fear as those eerie screams pursued them for what seemed an age. □

They had just reached what the old man called 'stall-shit corner' — a spot below a group of stables apparently — when it happened.

There was the clatter of a sewer cover being lifted and dropped on to the cobbles of the road above. '*Freeze everybody!*' Shit Thomas hissed with surprising energy for such an old man.

They froze. Alarmed and frightened, they pressed their bodies against the dripping walls of the sewer, hardly daring to breathe as a thin beam of cold light cut the gloom of the sewer above them.

'*Die sind da — ganz bestimmt!*' Jerzy heard a harsh, determined voice bark in German. '*Ich weiss das genau.*'

Apparently the man who had spoken had not convinced his comrades that there was anyone in the tunnel, for one of them said, 'Oh, Kurt, you'll be seeing Polacks in yer sleep next. There ain't one of those shit eaters within a kilometre from here. They're all up in the Old City getting their stupid Polack turnips blown off, mate.'

Jerzy swallowed hard and ducked as the thin beam passed the spot where his head had been a moment before. Would the Fritz be convinced he was wrong?

He wasn't.

'I'll give the place a squirt with...'

Jerzy could not hear the rest of the words; they were drowned by the sound of something metallic being dropped to the cobbles. He bit his bottom lip and wondered what the Fritzes were up to. The light flicked off, leaving him blinking hurriedly, trying to accustom his eyes again to the gloom.

There was the sound of a match being struck. Across on the other side of the sewer, the old man threw him an enquiring look. Jerzy shrugged. He didn't know either what was going on above.

Jerzy started suddenly. Above them there was a frightening hiss and even at the distance they were from the Germans, he could feel the sudden heat. Across the way the old man's face blanched as he realized in the same instant what was going on.☐

'Run for it!' Jerzy screamed. 'They're gonna use a flame-thrower!' He pulled out his pistol and fired a burst blindly up the hole. There was a scream, the sound of someone falling heavily and in a flash, panic swept through the sewer, with men and women fleeing past the young Pole, screaming as they ran.

'Get a hold of them!' Jerzy yelled above the panic-stricken cries. '*Get them on the way, Shit Thomas!*' He grabbed the English

Sten gun off the back of a running man, as he dashed by. 'I'll deal with it.'

The flame-thrower roared. An angry tongue of blue-red flame hissed into the sewer, curling around the walls, making them glow momentarily, seeking out its prey, finding it and burning the flesh off the screaming victims. Jerzy ducked, feeling the tremendous heat sear his back, his nostrils abruptly full of the stench of charred flesh. Next moment he was fighting his way across the blackened mess of horribly burnt bodies, clambering up the dripping ladder, knowing that he was going to his death, but consumed by such a rage that he went willingly...

The colonel pressed the trigger. The slugs splattered against the wall. He could see the little bits of stone erupting from the bricks quite clearly. The Fritz who barred their way ducked. The burst missed. But it did the trick all the same. The Fritz flung away his rifle and bolted down the road, swinging round the corner before the colonel could snap another magazine into his pistol.

At his side Sergeant Griska laughed, his eyes gleaming wildly with the madness of battle. 'Fanny's drawers for you, colonel!' he yelled above the crackle of small arms' fire. 'They'd never have let you out of recruit training in my day!' He raised his rifle and snapped off a single shot.

The sniper, who had just drawn a bead on the big officer standing in the middle of the alley, threw up his arms, his rifle clattering to the cobbles, and slumped over the sill, dead.

The colonel laughed too. 'What does it matter. *Nitchevo!* As long as I've got gulag rats like Sergeant Griska!... Come on.' He grabbed the wall and heaved.

Sergeant Griska followed and the two of them crouched there, firing into the German-occupied houses on both sides, while the other rats scaled the wall, taking casualties all the time, so that the base of the wall was soon littered with dead and wounded Russians. The last rats were able to climb up the human ladder and ran to take their positions among the bushes in the gardens on the other side.

'Off you go, master shot!' the colonel yelled and pushed Griska.

He toppled to the ground, while the colonel remained there, firing all the time, but trying also to assess what lay before them in the 300 metres or so which separated the survivors from the exit to the sewer. And then just as he dropped to the ground, he caught a quick glimpse of the squat shape that was swinging round the corner to their front. His heart sank. It was a Fritz tank. *The way to the sewer was barred once more!*

Vassily saw the tank at virtually the same time as the Old Man did. He and his men had had an easy passage along the bank. Perhaps the fact that the old Man's group had been spotted and involved in a running fight had drawn off the Fritzes who might have attacked his own. He didn't know, nor did he care. All that concerned him now was that the Old Man's group was bogged down and didn't stand a chance in hell of getting past the German Mark IV, which had buried itself in the ruins of one of the houses in a hull-down position, its machine-guns scything its immediate front, making it a death trap.

'Sergeant,' he cried over his shoulder to his senior NCO, 'get the men moving again. Take the street to your left. You'll see the exit to the sewer there — a kind of ornate cellar facade, that's how it was described to me. Form a perimeter around it, and hold on to it for God's sake!'

'Yes, comrade captain. And you?'

'Don't worry about me. I'm gonna do a little tank hunting. Off you go. *Davoi!*'

The NCO didn't wait for any further explanation. He wanted no part of tackling a Fritz tank with no better weapon than an infantry carbine and a pistol, which were all that the captain was armed with. '*Davoi!*' he growled at his men. 'Move out — at the double now!'

Vassily waited till they had cleared the street and disappeared round the bend, noting that there was no sound of firing from that direction; then he took another look at the situation which confronted him.

The tank was buried almost up to its turret in brick rubble, its rump protected by a solid wall, so there was no hope of tackling it from that end. He eyed the turret. The Fritz tank commander must be an experienced bastard, he told himself, for he had buttoned the Mark IV completely. He obviously knew the old street fighter's trick of springing up on to the turret and pumping a swift volley into the open hatch.

Vassily bit his lip and knew, though he didn't want to, that there was only one way to tackle the Mark IV. He would have to blind it: somehow get round to its front, snap off a quick shot through the driver's slit and then blast every periscope he could see. But it was a lethal tactic. For the thirty or forty seconds he would be crouched there at the front, he would be in full view of every man in the tank, and at least two of them — the gunner and the tank commander — would be in a position to blast him to eternity with their machine-guns. It was simply a question of who would be able to react the quickest.

Vassily hesitated a moment, feeling fear trace a cold finger down his spine and his feet begin to root to the ground. He didn't want to. Let the Old Man and the rest of the gulag rats look after themselves. Wasn't he risking enough by attempting to hold the sewer exit while the unknown Poles escaped? Why should he attempt the impossible?

Abruptly he recalled Vulf's solemn words to him after he had told the little ex-intellectual that he had just convinced the CO to go into Praga: 'Vassily, you should be proud of yourself. You have done something that even the great Stalin never dared do. *You have sentenced the Old Man to death!*' He knew then that he had to attempt it.

Hastily he unslung the rifle and taking his pistol out of its holster, thrust it into the front of his belt. He drew a deep breath, counted up to three and then he was out in the open, doubling towards the rear of the tank. He knew that the crew inside could not hear his approach because of the racket kicked up by the chattering machine-gun. He was safe enough — at the moment. He drew parallel with the turret, ducked below the thirty-degree range of the turret periscopes and, bent double, came to the front bogie of the tank. There he dropped to the brick-littered ground and crawled to the front, feeling the heat of the machine-guns pounding away in the turret as he did so.

Almost at once the fire from the other side — where the gulag rats had gone to ground — died away and he knew they had seen him and had guessed what he was attempting to do. But he had no time to look; his whole attention was concentrated on crawling round without being spotted by the driver who was now less than half a metre away from him.

He breathed out a sigh of relief. He had done it! He was in position. He rested there a moment, his heart thudding away, his body lathered in sweat, desperately trying to control himself, steel himself for what he must do. Not taking his eyes away one instant from the steel monster which towered above him, he clicked off the safety on his rifle, then on the pistol.

Again he counted three. 'NOW!' he screamed as he sprang to his feet. He caught the blur of white and the sudden startled look in the pair of eyes which peered out at him from the slit in the driver's compartment and pumped three shots at the opening. The first two howled off the metal harmlessly. The third slammed right through the slit. A white blur flooded bright crimson and the chatter of the machine-guns above could not drown that terrible scream.

He dropped the rifle. The machine-gunner was frantically trying to depress his weapon to slaughter this lone Russian who had appeared so abruptly from nowhere. Vassily whipped out his pistol and fired. His first shot shattered the gunner's telescope and the first machine-gun stopped immediately. Vassily aimed at the left-hand periscope. His slug whined off the edge of the turret. Desperately Vassily fired again. There was the satisfying sound of crystal smashing and abruptly the turret M.G. went dead. He had done it! He had paralysed the tank and he still lived. *He had done it!*

Trembling in every limb, he dropped the pistol from nerveless fingers, his shoulders slumped as if he were exhausted. Slowly he turned. 'Comrades,' he called in a voice that he hardly recognized as his own, 'it's safe now… You can advance… *Davoi*…'

Weakly he grinned as the first cautious heads appeared above the walls and bushes. He spotted the Old Man and waved again, 'Come on, colonel. The Fritz sardine can is done for. The way is —'

'*Vassily!*' the colonel's tremendous bellow and the look on his face told him that something had gone wrong.

He swung round.

The turret hatch had been thrown back. A German in the black uniform of the tank corps stood swaying there, his face a gory red mess, as if someone had thrown a handful of strawberry jam at it. Where his eyes had once been there were two suppurating, scarlet pits. In his hands he clutched a Schmeisser machine pistol and he was babbling crazily as he swung it to and fro, seeking the man who had done this terrible thing to him. For one long moment Vassily was rooted to the spot, mesmerized by that horrible apparition. Then the shouts of the gulag rats alarmed him to his danger. Blind as he was, the dying German above him in the turret could not miss. He must run!

'*Run!... Run!*' a half a hundred fear-crazed voices urged him.

Vassily turned and started to run, zig-zagging violently as he did so. The blind German heard the sound his running feet made and guessed it was the man he sought. He pressed the trigger. The Schmeisser chattered wildly at his side. Vassily zig-zagged just in time. The burst ripped along the length of the wall to his right.

'*Hit the dirt!*' the colonel called desperately and, pulling out his own pistol, loosed off a wild salvo at the German in the turret. Vassily didn't hear. He was driven on by an overwhelming, unreasoning fear of the man he had blinded that made him forget everything save that he must reach the safety of the gulag rats. He must! The German's machine pistol chattered once. Again he missed. Now Vassily was only thirty odd metres away from the gulag rats. In spite of the danger from the flying bullets, they were on their feet, all of them, their faces set, white and tense, fists clenched painfully, willing him to reach them safely. He was going to do it.

The German fired for the last time. Vassily screamed shrilly. He stopped in mid-stride, his hand frantically clawing the air, the burning pain exploding the length of his back. He had been hit. Slowly, as the German behind him slumped dead over the edge of the turret, the Schmeisser clattering useless now to the deck, Vassily went down on to his knees, fighting off death with all the strength he still had left. Red and white lights exploded in front of his eyes. He felt his head lolling from one side to the other like that of a drunk. Hot, salty blood flooded his mouth. 'I won't … won't die…' he gurgled as he sensed the earth reaching up to embrace him. 'Won't … die…'

The sewer was beginning to grow larger and cooler. The water mixed with the sludge through which they trudged was suddenly quite cold. 'The Vistula,' the old man explained.

'*The Vistula!*' the name went from mouth to mouth, till it became an echo in the far reaches of the sewer. '*The Vistula!*' They had nearly done it.

Thin grey light began to flood into the shaft, illuminating the rats that scurried hither and thither. There was a constant shower of water from above now. 'Surprised the old sod has held this long,' the old man chuckled. 'Must be at least a couple of hundred years old. Doubt if it'll survive much longer.'

The young woman at his side shivered and looked up apprehensively.

'Don't worry, miss. It'll last till we get out, no doubt,' the old man said. 'You'll be safe till you get out up there and face the Fritzes.'

Five minutes later the old man halted to face what appeared to be a solid, heavy oak grating. Behind him there came dismal groans as the escapers thought they had run into an insurmountable barrier.

The old man chuckled again. With his little finger he lifted the grating out of its mounting and said, 'Balsa wood. Made special by the *kanalarki* to fool the Fritzes. Come on, we're going up now.'

They started to emerge from the ornate entrance of the sewer, blinking in the bright light of the morning, staring apprehensively at the gulag rats, ragged, dirty, some of them already drunk on looted German schnaps. In their turn, they regarded these young men and women, many of whom had big blue-bottles buzzing around their maggot-filled bandages, as if they were creatures from another world.

Propped up against a shattered wall, Vassily watched with the little strength still left to him from his fatal wound. The colonel, together with Sergeant Griska, had tried to stem the blood flowing from the gaping hole in his back, packing it full of rags. When they were immediately soaked they applied a thick mud poultice while Vassily screamed with unbearable pain. But all had been no good. Griska, wiping his hands clean of the bloody gore on the grass, had whispered, 'Gut haemorrhage, colonel. Seen it all before. He ain't got a chance. It's the angels for him now, comrade.' And the colonel had given in, knowing that the grizzled NCO was right; Vassily was doomed to die.

Now the young Polish officer was fading rapidly. His cheeks had taken on that sunken look, the end of the nose pinched and pointed, which always indicated the swiftly approaching end. Yet Vassily feasted his weary eyes on the Poles scattering into the ruins, breaking purposefully into little groups, heading for the outskirts and Praga, for freedom. It was as if it were vitally important to him to survive till the last one had safely passed through. Finally there was no one left save the old man, who stared at the dying officer, cap in gnarled hands, curious, yet in no way apparently moved.

Vassily raised his head and with the last of his strength cried in his own language, '*Long live Poland!*' Next instant a thick flow of bright red blood shot from his mouth, his head lolled to one side and he was dead. Opposite him the old man silently crossed himself in the elaborate Polish fashion, replaced his cap on his cropped head and slowly, thoughtfully, started to walk back to the sewer.

CHAPTER 3

At eight o'clock on the evening of 2 October, 1944, Warsaw finally surrendered after sixty-three days of the bitterest fighting. Over the next twenty-four hours, the beaten Poles were allowed to evacuate civilians from the worst-hit districts of the capital.

A dreadful silence hung over the smoking heaps of rubble which had once been the Old City and the shattered suburbs. Hollow-eyed, ragged men and women of the Home Army waited for their last order from Bor.

It came, and it was hard. They were to march into German captivity after handing over their weapons. There would be no exception. He, Bor, expected the strictest obedience from them. They would march to the Kerceli Square on the fourth and surrender their weapons to the waiting Germans; thereafter they were to move to the suburb of Wola where the enemy would have transport ready to take them to the POW camps. It was the end.

Kass and Dirlewanger were among the many high-ranking German officers who waited that grey October day for the Poles. They came in the mid-morning, singing, and it was their song that the Germans heard first. Kass could not understand the text, but as hard and as insensitive as he was, the sound of those words ringing out from many thousand throats brought the tears to his eyes.

Not so Dirlewanger. He understood Polish. He threw down his cigarette and ground it angrily under his heel. 'The insolent Polack swine,' he cried. 'They have the audacity to sing their national song — *Not Yet Is Poland Lost.*'

But this day no one was listening to the saturnine-faced sadist. Their ears full of that bold, sad song, they stared as a man at the beaten Poles as they swung round the corner, filling the ruined street from side to side.

Most of them, men and women, were wounded, parched with thirst and starving, yet they kept their step, their heads high and proud, eyes fixed firmly on some distant horizon, as if they were not aware that they were now in the presence of the feared and hated enemy, who stared at the spectacle of this ragged, down-at-heel civilian army in open-mouthed amazement.

Next to Kass, his elegant chief-of-staff, the arch cynic gulped and clicked to attention, his hand raised to his gleaming peaked cap, and suddenly Kass found himself doing the same, saluting those men and women, who only days before he had tried to wipe off the face of the earth.

Furious and trembling with suppressed rage, Dirlewanger turned and strode away, slashing his elegant boots with his riding crop, unable to bear the sight of the Polacks being treated like this. So it was that he did not see the rank after rank of set faces, the steady tramp of boots, the sobs from the handful of tearful Polish civilians who had ventured out to see their fighters march into captivity: a captivity from which most would never return. For even those who survived the German camps were no longer welcome in the country for which they had shed their blood. The new masters in Warsaw did not want their kind of Pole back home. They would spread all over the western world, like the Jews of old, from the nineteenth century industrial cities of Yorkshire and Lancashire to the bustling concrete jungles of Chicago and Pittsburgh, to become embittered old men and women, speaking a strange tongue and reading obscure newspapers, cut off from their neighbours, living in a past that had vanished for good that summer of 1944...

But Dirlewanger took his revenge for the insult of that October day. Now on the Führer's express order, the killers who had survived the battle — and Dirlewanger had lost nearly half his effectives during the fight for Warsaw — swarmed into the centre of the capital, to carry out their bloody task.

While special squads of the Dirlewangers searched the ruins for what they could find to loot, the rest set about the systematic destruction of what was left of Warsaw. Polish civilians were forced at gunpoint to drill holes into the walls of the buildings to be destroyed, others followed them packing in the long sausages of gelignite and fusing them. A third group lit the fuses and ran for their lives for the Dirlewangers were mostly too drunk to calculate the right time sequence.

Like barbarians of old, armed with the deadly tools of the twentieth century, the Dirlewangers proceeded from street to street. Schools, museums, factories, palaces, hospitals, buildings historic, buildings ordinary, all were destroyed. But it did not just stop there. Parks were set afire by flame-throwers. Ornamental lakes and ponds filled in with brick rubble. The sewer system destroyed so that the streets ran with human excrement, flooding the graves and the cellars in which lay the dead, a quarter of a million of them.

Then it was all over. Warsaw had been destroyed like no other city in the twentieth century. It presented a picture of sordid horror. The streets were blocked with great crazy heaps of rubble, the steel skeletons of the buildings twisted into impossible grotesque shapes, with the tortured bodies of the dead lying everywhere; and over it all hung the great stench that drove the Dirlewangers out finally: a stench composed of decaying bodies and the sickly sweet smell of escaping gas, plus the overpowering odour of excrement. It was the stench of death.

On the same day that the Dirlewangers finally completed their task of destruction and fled the charnel house, the 2nd White Russian Army broke through to Praga.

By that time the gulag rats had been reduced to some 200 effectives, old men who shuffled bleary-eyed towards their rescuers in rags, their boots flapping and broken-soled, croaking weakly the old cry, '*Slava krasnaya armya!*'

'Long live the Red Army,' the newcomers returned the traditional greeting, their eyes full of amazement. Could these human skeletons be the men who had held off the Fritzes for so long? *Could they?* On the same day, while the colonel and his surviving NCOs and senior officers were celebrating by eating their first good meal for a month, resisting the temptation to wolf down the hot food like the starving animals they had become these last terrible weeks, a civilian car drove up to the bullet-marked HQ.

Through the shattered window the colonel noted the green crosses on the caps of the two NCOs who got out of it. NKVD, he told himself, and dismissing the matter, concentrated on the juicy slice of pork, dripping with thick garlic gravy.

But not for long.

Imperiously the splintered door to the HQ was thrown open. The two NKVD NCOs stood there, stony-faced and hard-eyed. They wasted no words. Swinging their gaze along the line of ragged officers and NCOs, they demanded in that arrogant manner of the NKVD, which suggested that a sergeant was more important than a general of the Red Army, 'Which of your scum is the commander?'

The colonel pushed back his packing case seat and rose slowly to his feet, noting as he did so the fear printed all too clearly on the faces of his fellow officers. 'Who are you? What do you want?' he demanded.

His tone had no effect on the two NCOs. It was not the first time they had arrested a senior officer and it wouldn't be the last.

'On the orders of the Stavka, approved by Marshal Rokossovsky you are placed under arrest forthwith,' the bigger of the two barked, one hand on his pistol, the other waving a slip of paper at the ragged, emaciated colonel.

'Arrest ... why?'□

'We're not here to answer questions,' the other man said. 'Are you coming peacefully or —'

'Damn your eyes, you swine,' Vulf blurted out, pushing back his case and overturning it, his pale face flushed crimson, 'what right have you rear echelon pigs to come bursting in here and —'

The colonel silenced the little officer with a quick glance. He knew that there was no hope for him, although he had held off the Fritzes for six bloody weeks. His fate had already been decided in Moscow. Why involve the others? Quietly he walked forward to the waiting secret policemen and held out his wrists, his fists suddenly clenched.

The bigger of the two snapped home the handcuffs and attached them to the chain which dangled from his own wrist. He tugged hard to check whether the device worked. It did. The colonel let his shoulders sag in defeat. Now it was all over.

'*Bosche moi!*' a captain cried angrily and tossed down his fork noisily. An NCO sobbed. But all of them present there knew and feared the power of the NKVD. There was no fighting back against them. They were the real and only power in the Soviet state.

Arrogantly, so confident of their power over these ragged gulag rats who had shed their blood so often for a state that despised them, they led their captive to the waiting car, the driver gunning his engine as if he could not wait to take the prisoner to his well-earned fate — death.

Passing through the door, the colonel heard Sergeant Griska's last words as he speared another piece of dripping pork with his trench knife, 'I doubt, comrades, if we'll be seeing the Old Man ever again. Eat up. This pork is really good!'

The colonel smiled faintly and told himself that Griska was a realist ... his words seemed as fitting an epitaph for a gulag rat as any...

CHAPTER 4

The trial, if it could be called that, was held in an abandoned schoolroom in Praga, with the sound of the guns rumbling outside as sombre background music. Under other circumstances the heavy-set generals of the panel, crouched awkwardly in the desks meant for ten-year-olds, might have seemed slightly ludicrous, but not now. For the generals' panel had already been given their orders by the undersized, bespectacled NKVD lieutenant, who was the real power behind the trial, and it read — *death*. The general did not like the order one bit; after all the man they were going to sentence to death was one of their own; but hard, brutal, powerful men though they were, they still trembled in the presence of the mild-mannered NKVD lieutenant. Their broad soldiers' faces gloomy, they crouched there absurdly, and wished privately that it would all be over soon, and they could hurry back to the cleaner, more wholesome world of the fighting front.

The prosecutor, a fat colonel who affected a pince-nez in the fashion of Beria, the Head of the NKVD, began the trial in a business-like, no-nonsense manner, reading out the accusation in a firm, determined voice as if no sensible, honest man could doubt, in the slightest, the truth of his words. 'The prisoner was given a specific order by Marshal of the Soviet Union Rokossovsky personally,' he glanced briefly at the marshal, who sat in the centre of the panel at the schoolmaster's desk, looking moodily at the children's drawings which lined the room. 'He was commanded not to contact the Polish fascist insurgents in any way. The prisoner paid no attention to that order. Instead he enabled several hundreds of the fascists to escape at the cost of two score Russian soldiers' lives. Those Polish fascists have so far managed to evade capture.' He threw a quick look at the bespectacled NKVD officer who was doodling on his pad. The latter nodded. 'And it appears that they are now at liberty to continue their illegal campaign against the Red Army and the Polish authorities duly and legally appointed by Comrade Secretary Stalin,' he said the words as if they were in quotes.

He grunted and cleared his throat. 'How do you plead, prisoner?' he rapped, looking at the shaven-headed gulag rat, who was still dressed in the ragged, mud-stained uniform he had worn during the long battle to hold Praga, as if he were seeing him for the first time and didn't like what he saw.

The colonel blinked through his puffed-up eyes, seeing the court through a red-rimmed mist, only able to half-catch the prosecutor's words for his ears were still blocked with congealed blood. Of course the NKVD had beaten him; he had expected it. The NKVD lieutenant had conducted the beating personally and had displayed surprising strength for such a weedy little man. The night before he had come into the colonel's miserable cell, accompanied by the bigger of the two NCOs who had arrested him. They had placed a pail on the hamstrung prisoner's head and the lieutenant had commenced smashing a broom-handle against the pail crying, *'We will confess our guilt … we'll not answer back … we will go tamely to our death…'* until the blood had erupted from his smashed nostrils and ruptured eardrums and he had fallen to the bloody floor in a faint.

The prosecutor repeated his demand: 'How do you plead, prisoner, guilty or not guilty?'

Still the prisoner did not answer.

The prosecutor flushed angrily. 'Damn you, man, answer, will you? Or I'll have the knout taken to you!'

The little lieutenant cleared his throat noisily in warning. The prosecutor got the message. 'Well?' he asked in a more normal voice. □

'I ... I kill Germans,' the colonel croaked in a worn voice, full of pain. 'I hold ... Praga ... I give the Red Army the ... the bridges it needed...'

Opposite him Marshal Rokossovsky bit his bottom lip and stared deliberately at the yellowing photograph of some local nineteenth-century worthy, as if he could not bear to look at the tortured face of the man who had once been his comrade in the camps. Other generals on the panel cleared their throats in embarrassment. *They* knew only too well what sacrifices the gulag rats had made to hold the left bank of the *Vistula*. Only the little lieutenant seemed unmoved by the prisoner's outburst. He had heard the same kind of thing often enough before. He started to clean his long nails with his pocket knife.

'I am not interested in that in the least,' the colonel rapped. 'Let us have your answer to this simple single question — did you help the Polish fascists to escape from the capital?'

It was not the colonel who answered the question, but Marshal of the Soviet Union Konstantin Rokossovsky. 'Of course, he's damned guilty, colonel!' he roared suddenly, his pale, cunning face flushed with rage, sick of the prisoner, the prosecutor, the panel, the whole fake business. 'Let's put an end to this farce! Why am I forced to waste my time here. Am I not the commander of a whole army engaged at a time when the enemy front is breaking down everywhere? I am needed at my headquarters to direct operations.' He glared at the NKVD lieutenant, who was showing surprise for the first time since he had entered the schoolroom, his nails forgotten now. 'What the devil am I doing here being forced to deal with this rat from the Gulag, eh?' He stared around the assembled officers, his chest heaving with the effort of his outburst. 'I demand a sentence *now*, immediately and an end to this whole absurd business!'

The prosecutor looked appealingly at the NKVD lieutenant. He nodded, suddenly deflated by the marshal's angry tirade.

'*Horoscho*, comrades,' the prosecutor said hastily, glad to be relieved of any further responsibility for what might result from the manner in which the court-martial was now being conducted. 'Let us vote on the verdict.' Hastily the generals scribbled their verdict on the pieces of paper set out in readiness before them, one or two of them hesitating but only because they needed the time to fish out the spectacles they never dared wear publicly, to scrawl their verdict and signature, before passing the papers up to the waiting president of the court, who was drumming his manicured fingers impatiently on the schoolmaster's desk.

Rokossovsky did not even deign to look at them. He knew what the verdict was already. With an angry gesture he swept them to one side, his mind abruptly filled with a picture of his old comrade entering his hut with a bowl of steaming porridge the time when he, Rokossovsky, had typhus. No one else had dared come within fifty metres of him in case they were infected by the terrible disease, but the colonel had fed him with the wooden spoon like a baby. He dismissed the old memory. 'Prisoner,' he barked harshly. 'You have been found guilty of disobeying an order given to you by a superior officer. Not only that, you have also disobeyed a specific command of Comrade Stalin and have endangered the security of the Soviet Union. What have you to say?' The colonel looked at him through narrowed eyes, opened his mouth to reveal the toothless gums (they had taken away the stainless steel teeth), then thought better of it. He shook his head slowly.

'*Horoscho!*' Marshal Rokossovsky snapped, obviously relieved. 'The sentence of this court is death.' Hastily he rose to his feet. The others followed suit awkwardly, the little NKVD man beaming happily. '*Court dismissed!*'

A moment later he swept out, followed by the generals, without a single look at the bent-shouldered gulag rat, who was now abandoned to his fate...

And far away that night in Moscow, the pock-marked, swarthy Georgian puffed his curved pipe contentedly, the two messages brought by the hunchbacked secretary spread out on his knee. The one informed him that Warsaw was his. It had fallen into his lap like a ripe plum; the Poles had done his work for him, the fools. The second message was of lesser importance, yet it gave a similar feeling of satisfaction. It read simply. '*Execution Commander 333 Punishment Battalion carried out this morning, as ordered. Rokossovsky.*'

'You are pleased, comrade?' Aleksander Proskrebyshev whined, wringing his hands as if they were very dirty, an old habit of his when he was in the presence of the dictator, no one knew why.

'I *am* pleased, comrade,' Stalin said, puffing again at his pipe, his old-fox eyes at rest for once. 'Things are going well. God is in his heaven, as the *kulaks* used to say, and all is well with the world. Even the gulag rats fear me now.'

'Soon the whole world will fear you, comrade,' the hunchbacked secretary suggested, a fawning look on his yellow face.

'Perhaps, comrade, perhaps,' Stalin sucked reflectively at his pipe, as he warmed to the thought. 'But fear is the key, Poskrebyshev, fear.' He pointed his pipe at the secretary and suddenly the dictator's dark eyes blazed. '*The knout*, that is the only thing that human beings understand!'

The secretary trembled, as he recognized the infinite cruelty which shone in the unblinking little eyes of the man who would one day rule Europe…

BOOK FOUR: *ENVOI*

CHAPTER 1

It was snowing now, great soft wet flakes which muffled the thunder of the guns that heralded the great new Russian offensive into the Reich itself. Standing in long lines, leaning on their weapons, their breath congealing on the freezing air in little grey clouds, the gulag rats of the newly reformed 333rd Punishment Battalion waited patiently, the snow forming white mantles on their shoulders. There was little chatter, although they were standing at ease; for each man was preoccupied with his own thoughts this January day, motivated by the knowledge that they would soon be leading the assault into Germany proper.

To their front, glimpsed through the falling snow, the big colonel standing in the middle of the HQ staff cars, finished unfurling the great red flag and stamped through the snow to where the gulag rats waited.

Major Pavlov, the acting battalion commander, snapped an order. As one, the thousand-odd men of the Punishment Battalion clicked to attention.

The colonel halted and Pavlov swept up his gleaming silver sabre and saluted the colonel and the flag. Behind him Vulf nodded to the youngest officer in the battalion, a seventeen-year-old under-lieutenant, who had been sent to the Gulag for chalking anti-Stalin slogans on the wall of his school at the age of fourteen. Proudly the handsome youth, who had been attracting Vulf's attention ever since he had been posted to the battalion, marched forward to face the colonel with the flag.

'Battalion — *battalion will kneel!*' Pavlov commanded.

The gulag rats went down on one knee as the under-lieutenant did the same and reaching up, took the tip of the red flag and pressed his lips to it.

Sternly the staff colonel read out the new oath that Stalin had insisted that all his soldiers who were now to enter Germany were to swear to the flag. 'I swear on my honour as a citizen of the USSR, a communist, and a soldier of the Red Army that I will do my duty for Mother Russia, for...'

Standing next to the staff cars, fur collar pulled up high against the snowflakes, cigarette in one corner of his mouth and his fur cap tilted at a rakish angle, Marshal Rokossovsky nudged his companion and said cynically. 'It is a scene from the days of the czars, little brother. All we need now is the pope going through the ranks like a great black crow splashing holy water all over the place.'

His companion, a harshly handsome man with a bitter mouth, nodded his agreement. 'But it serves a purpose, brother. Soon we will enter Germany and the west. The temptations there are tenfold what they have been here in Poland. There could be desertions and Old Leather Face knows that.'

'Yes, you are right. Now he wishes to bind them to the idea of a great patriotic war being fought for Russia and *not* for those crooks in Moscow.' The Marshal blew out a stream of angry blue smoke.

'*I swear by our flag!*' a thousand hoarse voices roared and then the Punishment Battalion was shuffling to its feet.

Marshal Rokossovsky threw away his cigarette. 'Come,' he commanded.

Together the two tall officers stamped through the streaming snow to where the gulag rats waited to receive their new commander before they marched west into the unknown.

The marshal took the lead, halting next to the staff colonel who held the fluttering blood-red banner which he hated from the bottom of his soul. 'I shall not speak long,' he cried so that the men in the rear rank could hear him above the thunder of the guns. 'I was once a front swine myself. I know what it is like to freeze one's eggs off listening to some pomaded, pompous fool from a rear HQ spout shit.'

There were suppressed laughs from the gulag rats; the marshal was living up to his reputation of speaking the earthy language of his soldiers.

'Today you march west across the borders of the fascist enemy. Today we strike the first blow which will bring down the Fritz empire like a house of cards. Today you begin the *last* campaign.'

Rokossovsky allowed them a moment to absorb the implications of that 'last' campaign.

'Undoubtedly some of you will be wounded. Undoubtedly some of you will be killed on the field of battle, and equally undoubtedly being the gulag rats you are, some of you will be tempted to desert and enjoy the Fritz fleshpots.' His voice hardened. '*Don't!*' His hard blue eyes swept the long ranks of soldiers so that here and there a man shivered, and it was not on account of the cold.

'I shall tell you why. On my honour as a marshal of the Soviet Union, I promise you here and now that those of you who survive the great battle to come will never see the inside of the Gulag again. That is my solemn promise. There will be no more Gulag Archipelago!'

Not giving the surprised gulag rats time to consider how he might bring about that tremendous feat, while Stalin was still alive, the marshal rapped. 'Here is your new commander who will lead you to victory and freedom.' He swung round. 'Colonel Kristos!'

Kristos! Vulf caught the name but could not yet quite make out the features of the man striding to the front of the battalion in the imperious way of a soldier used to command. It sounded Greek; he had never heard of a Russian of that name, nor even a Ukrainian for that matter. Suddenly he gasped as the snowflakes parted a little and he got a clear look at the harshly handsome face of the new commander. Hastily his hand flew to his mouth to prevent himself from crying out his name.

Sergeant Griska did not manage it. '*Bosche moi*!' he exclaimed, eyes wide with surprise. '*It's the Old Man ... come back from the dead...*'

'Of course,' Vulf told himself, '*Kristos was Christ*! Like Jesus.' Rokossovsky, the cunning dog, had resurrected him somehow or other.

The new commander, Colonel Kristos, did not seem to notice that his reappearance was having such an effect upon the gulag rats. His face set and non-committal, he barked: '*333 Punishment Battalion — Battalion atten-SHUN*!'

Awkwardly, still not recovered from the tremendous surprise, the gulag rats shuffled to attention.

Colonel Kristos swung round and smartly raised his hand in salute.

The marshal returned it with a smile on his lips, and for one long moment the two old gulag rats faced each other, with the colonel willing the other man to comprehend his overwhelming gratitude for the way in which he had staged the mock execution (a German spy) for the benefit of the NKVD lieutenant, how he had kept him hidden for nearly three months until a suitable time had elapsed and proper documents had been acquired to equip him for his new role as Colonel Kristos, the resurrected one. Then he barked, 'Permission to march, comrade marshal?'

'Permission to march granted, comrade colonel!' the marshal snapped and winked solemnly.

The colonel did not seem to notice. He turned and cried: 'Shoulder arms!'

The gulag rats executed the movement and he ordered them to turn before placing himself at the head of the long column, his sabre resting over his right shoulder.

The colonel's voice changed and suddenly there was warmth in it, as he was abruptly animated by the feeling that he was back with his own kind: the scum of the camps, the outcasts, the nameless ones whom Stalin had consigned to a speedy, violent death. 'The gulag rats,' he roared in a voice that the veterans remembered all too well, 'will advance. *Advance!*'

Five minutes later they had vanished into the whirling white fog, split here and there by the ugly scarlet flashes of gunfire, marching steadily westwards, heading for the last battle, determined to carve a new life out for themselves in the uncertain months to come in enemy Germany, heated by the heady new dream of freedom.

The gulag rats were on their way…

A NOTE TO THE READER

Dear Reader,
If you have enjoyed this novel enough to leave a review on **Amazon** and **Goodreads**, then we would be truly grateful.
Sapere Books

Sapere Books is an exciting new publisher of brilliant fiction and popular history.

To find out more about our latest releases and our monthly bargain books visit our website:
saperebooks.com